Second Chance
at
Christmastime

TERRY GARRETT

Second Chance at Christmastime

© 2021 Terry Garrett

Paperback ISBN: 978-1-66780-214-5

Prologue

L ined up alphabetically in pairs, wearing graduation caps and gowns over tee shirts and shorts, the Beacon High graduating class stood under a cerulean blue sky, prepared to proceed into the gymnasium. One hundred and fifty-two classmates ready for commencement. Kate Nola was in the middle of the pack and looked around at her friends. When she stood on her tiptoes and looked several rows behind her she could spot Chris Spring in one of the back rows. The blond ponytail of her bestie Jenny bobbed up and down as she chatted with the boy that stood next to her. Andy was running in late. He was so easy going, she wasn't surprised to see him hurrying in to get in position. She knew Dan was a few rows in front of her, but couldn't find him from where she was positioned. Kate thought about the word "commence." Wasn't it ironic to end thirteen years together, graduating from everyone and everything their world had ever been, to talk about beginnings instead of endings? She herself was hyper-focused on the ending. She didn't want it to end because her future plans were filled with uncertainty, unlike so many of her friends. She found herself playing with the fabric of her gown, dropping it to keep it from wadding into a wrinkle, then twirling her light brown hair in between her fingers instead. Shifting her weight from side to side, she tried to quell her nervousness.

A few rows ahead of her, Dan Ivy, her boyfriend of the past four years was lined up as well with confusing thoughts of his own. He had bitten his fingernails to the quick and beyond as some of them were raw. Wishing the graduation gown had pockets, he tried to still his hands. Now they felt clammy. The next step was sweaty. Great. He had been a Duke fan for as long as he could remember, and was thrilled at his acceptance, but as much as he felt excited about his future at Duke, he knew he would find it strange and unwelcome to be away from Kate. He consoled himself with the thought that Kate would only be a little over a two-hour drive away. It wouldn't be the same but he could still see her every weekend. And before they knew it, they would be together for Thanksgiving and Christmas.

As May turned to June and June to July and July to August, the summer flew by and it was time for the two of them to part ways. For the first time in their lives, they would not live a few blocks from each other. His world was expanding and she wasn't going to be a daily part of it anymore. And his idea of getting together every weekend wasn't going to happen for at least two months. She and her mom were now going to California.

The summer had flown by, maybe faster than any of the summers that came before. It was already time to say goodbye. As Dan and Kate embraced, it was hard for either of them to let go. They had never thought they would.

Ten Years Later

Chapter 1

Kate slipped into her favorite coral tennis shoes and threw a light blue denim jacket over her yoga clothes. She peeked around a corner of the studio, "Bye, Mom. I'll see you in a couple of hours to plan the village Christmas party. And please remember to change out the towels in the wash today." The Monday before Thanksgiving finally here, Kate was gearing up for her favorite weeks of the year, the time between Thanksgiving and Christmas so magically filled with holiday activities. Her mom stood barefoot behind the counter as she prepared an email blast to send out to their students, "Sorry hon. I know I forgot them the other day. Won't let it happen today." She looked younger than her fifty-three years, petite, fit, barefaced with no need for makeup, she ran a hand through her tousled salt and pepper hair styled in a short pixie cut. Dressed in her long-sleeved white yoga top and loose-fitting yoga pants, she didn't even wear jewelry other than the colorful bracelets on her wrists.

Kate's four-year-old dog Freddie was lying lazily at her mom's feet behind the counter in his roomy dog bed. Over the years he had become the yoga studio's ambassador. An important member of their yoga community, he took his job seriously and greedily gobbled up the treats most students kept in their pockets for him. When there were no students in the lobby, he took advantage of the break and spread out in his spot for a snooze. Good thing he and Kate went for long runs most mornings so he could work off all the treats.

Every Monday Kate's alarm went off at five a.m. so she could teach her six o'clock class. One of the best things about her job was that once she rolled out of bed, got dressed, splashed some cold water on her face, and tossed her wavy light brown hair into a ponytail, she was ready to go. Freddie would run to her with his leash as soon as she put on her running shoes, if not before. She never left in the morning without the lucky dog at her side. When she opened the yoga studio and her faithful early morning students started to arrive, it felt normal to be up at the crack of dawn starting her day. She knew she was one of the fortunate ones who loved her work. She felt as good after teaching a class as she did when she took one. It must be all the steady breathwork and flowing movement.

Now twelve hours later she'd just taught her third class of the day. Monday was always the busiest day of the week with many of her students wanting to start off their week on a positive note after indulging in carefree weekends. And luckily her teaching schedule wasn't that full every day. She was grateful for the flexibility and the opportunity to work with her mom. There was nothing she'd rather do and she felt the usual gratitude rising in her heart for her life and the studio they owned together. For the better part of the past nine years, they had built a successful yoga business that she'd never dreamed would become her life. It was incredible to her that the only issues they ever had were minor. She was a neat freak, and well, let's just say her mom needed to be prodded every now and then to notice when something obvious to Kate needed doing. Maggie was more relaxed and the studio could only run well when they both paid attention to detail. They both tried hard to compromise, her mom working to keep things tidy, and Kate relaxing a bit on her expectations.

Almost a decade ago, it had felt like a pipe dream. Kate's mom had decided to give herself the gift of learning to become a yoga teacher. She wanted to be able to help others experience the way yoga made her feel.

Maggie had definitely come to believe the old adage that you can't pour from an empty cup so it was time for her to focus on herself, not something that came naturally to her. She had been amazed at the difference simply paying attention to breathing and staying in sometimes challenging postures could make, not just while she practiced yoga but throughout the rest of the day as well. She found it hard to explain to someone who hadn't experienced it, so she wanted to learn how to share it. Kate went to California with her, mostly because she didn't want to go to college, not yet having a clue of what she wanted to study. She and her mom had always been close, especially in the last couple of years when they only had each other. Kate also experienced amazing relief from yoga; even as a teen she had back pain and she felt such relief whenever she took a class.

So off they went. They spent the fall after she graduated high school traveling west to take a two-month training. The yoga teacher preparation was intense, but she felt alive and present and the further she and her mom immersed themselves into the program, the more inevitable it became that they would open a studio in Beacon once they completed their training. The days were long and tiring, but in the best possible way. She simultaneously felt spent and relaxed, and eventually, as each day ticked by, they both became more and more excited about the future.

Yoga taught Kate lessons that she hadn't learned anywhere else. Authenticity was a big one. She was only eighteen when she realized one of the biggest truths anyone can grasp. She was the only one who could be her. And she couldn't, nor would she want to be, anyone else. Everyone else was already taken anyway. But she wasn't. She had a role to play in the world, and it needed to fit only her. Then she could and would make a difference. She was also able to see what it had been like for her mom to live, not at all for herself, but for Kate and her father alone. It had been so exciting once her mom's eyes opened to the idea that she mattered too. Kate knew that lessons could be learned in various ways; she also knew that learning them on the yoga mat was a powerful way for them to sink in deeply.

While they were at the training, they often walked to the ocean's edge to watch the sunsets. One night they stayed up late, talking about the certifications they'd soon have and about the prospect of opening a studio of their own. Beacon didn't have a place to take classes and the charming village would offer a perfect location. As the plans that she and Maggie sketched for their dream studio back home started to come alive, Kate found herself excited about her own future. She was forgoing college with Dan, but it worked out fine really, since she hadn't had any idea of what she wanted to do career wise anyway. The only reason she had wanted to go to college at all had been to be with him, her high school sweetheart. Now that she had plans of her own, it seemed crazy that she would have made that choice. This was the career path for her, and if she and Dan were meant to be, they would make it work. She was young and starry-eyed, and she believed anything was possible.

Nine years had passed since Kate and Maggie had returned home, found an ideal location in the village with plenty of space to grow, and opened Beacon Yoga. Students trickled in slowly, mostly through word of mouth. Yoga was popular in nearby Charlotte, but that was the big city and transplants were flocking there from all over the country, many drawn to the area by banking and insurance companies taking advantage of the idyllic weather people didn't have in the Northeast that lured them southward.

In addition to the warmer weather, weekend retreats could be found a short three hours' drive northwest in the quaint mountain towns or three hours to the east on the beaches of the Atlantic.

As far as Maggie and Kate were concerned, there truly could not be a better place to live. North Carolina offered everything anyone could want. The way Beacon was growing, they had every reason to feel that way. So many of those who moved south had gone to yoga studios back home and searched out a new place to practice when they moved to Beacon. Some worked in Charlotte but liked the lifestyle afforded by a small town, but the only existing yoga studios were an inconvenient half hour away in the big city. Kate and Maggie wanted to provide a place for them where they could practice in their new hometown.

Before the growing population explosion, Beacon had been a different story, with a small-town population where most everyone had lived their entire lives and no one knew much about yoga. For the most part they were skeptical of something new. Maggie and Kate encouraged everyone they knew to at least give it a month, knowing most of them would be ready for yoga after just one class. Even so, the business grew slowly but steadily. The yoga space was far bigger than they needed when they opened, and they had been the only ones working there. The two of them put in long hours in that first year especially, and it ended up being healing for both of them. The list of tasks, however, was endless. At first, they taught all of the classes themselves, manned the front desk, filled the diffusers with aromatic oils, washed the lavender eye cloths and all the dirty towels they used to wipe down the floors after each class. A single eight o'clock morning class was offered that first year and Maggie taught it six days a week. Kate guided the six p.m. every day. Before they knew it, they needed another teacher to pick up a noon class, so they held their first teacher training to four interested students. Busy was good. Better than the alternative and kept their minds off the sadness and disappointments of the past. Nowadays the classes sometimes had wait lists and they needed new instructors often enough to offer a teacher training at least every other year.

Chapter 2

As Kate prepared to head home, she was unaware that her bubbly best friend Jenny was closing the sale on the empty café next door to none other than her high school sweetheart himself. Jenny and her husband Chris were Kate and Dan's best friends growing up. When Dan needed a realtor to help him find a location for the café that he came back home to open in Beacon, she was the natural choice. Clothed in her usual professional look of a sleeveless dress and matching blazer, today Jenny wore teal, and had paired the ensemble with comfortable black pumps. It seemed to her to be a little silly to dress up while with her old pal, but it was still work after all and it was important to dress the part.

Dan was dressed down compared to his stylish look of the past few years that he had spent working in the corporate world, but he was starting to feel like himself again in his comfortable khakis, long sleeved shirts rolled up at the cuffs, and casual loafers or boots. Boyishly handsome and a little over six feet tall, he wore his dark brown hair cropped short and had maintained a lean, fit physique. Returning home to Beacon after so many years away, he felt like even his skin fit again. He hadn't felt this confident or ready for a new venture in as long as he could remember. His life had taken a far different turn from Kate's once he went to college and didn't come home much, not even for school breaks or summers, mostly because of the strained relationship he had with his dad. He and his father never had thought alike on much of anything, and any real connection they might have had fell by the wayside when Dan's mom died. He had only been twelve, and that is a tough enough time in a boy's life. Navigating his teen years at home became even more difficult after that.

His dad had set high expectations for him but Dan's definition of success was far different from his father's. Dan had watched his dad throw himself into work, but he realized now that he never saw him happy or relaxed. His teenage years were good, though, mostly because of Kate and the time he spent at her house; her mom had provided a warm and welcoming place to hang out. Eventually after high school he and Kate had drifted apart; how and why it had happened he wasn't exactly sure. No that wasn't quite true. He knew precisely where to place the blame. He was the one who never came back home to Beacon.

"Dan, did you hear me? I was asking when you are going to let Kate know you are back." Jenny brushed a strand of straight blonde bangs out of her eyes as she questioned her friend. "It's been so hard keeping this from her so I hope you'll tell her soon." Jenny stared at him; her emerald green eyes filled with the kind of look that he knew meant business. Everyone always knew where they stood with her.

"I will Jenny. As soon as I get the chance. Or, you can tell her now that it is a done deal," his expression was hopeful. Watching him then stare at his shoes rather that look at her, she could tell he wasn't ready to see Kate yet. She wondered if he was frightened.

Actually, he was uneasy and would rather Jenny told her; he thought Kate might not find the idea of his being back to be a welcome thing, and he wasn't sure he could avoid looking hurt if her reaction was negative. He hardly ever wore his heart on his sleeve, but when it came to Kate, he probably still did.

"Okay, Dan, I've got to get going." She gave him a quick hug. "Chris and I are both so happy that you are back. Call or text if you need anything. And congrats again on the café. I'm happy for you. And us. And the village."

"Can't thank you enough, Jenny. Finding this location in the village, I am so excited about what I can offer here," he said as he returned the quick hug. Business dealings had not felt like this in New York.

A few minutes later Kate summoned Freddie to indicate that it was time to head home. "Let's go bud," she called out to him. She jingled his leash and he ran over, stubby tail wagging to go out on the short walk back to their house. Freddie was a purebred vizsla, and by nature they are highly active, almost hyperactive, fun loving, loyal dogs. Truly her sidekick, he was this woman's best friend.

Lost in thought, she didn't see the guy leaving the empty café until they collided on the sidewalk next to her studio, Freddie eagerly jumping up to greet the stranger.

"Oh, I'm sorry," she stammered as she lifted her gaze to--Dan! "I um, I didn't realize you were back in town," she exclaimed. "What brings you home this week, Thanksgiving? You haven't been home in, what, three or four years if memory serves me." What could he be doing here, she wondered? She couldn't help noticing how good he looked; clearly, he could still buy off the rack and the fit would work for him, his physique built for GQ. But that didn't matter anymore. They had been over for years and she wasn't about to get distracted by his familiar good looks.

He interrupted her thoughts. "Whoa, slow down Kate. I'm here because I'm buying the café. And who is this wonderful creature?" He gently pushed Freddie down off him and began petting him at the same time. Freddie nuzzled into the stranger; after all, his natural inclination was to serve as ambassador.

"What? I thought you were firmly ensconced in New York. Moving on up the ladder of success and following in your dad's footsteps." She tugged Freddie closer to her almost as if she needed a physical barrier between them. Forcing herself to stand taller, shaky as she felt, she didn't need him to see that. She projected strength on the outside, tiny as she was, but she was full of butterflies and jangly nerves on the inside.

His voice was soft. "Just because I went to Duke and started my life in corporate America doesn't mean I have to live like that forever. Wow, Kate. Give me a couple minutes to catch my breath. I've changed. I decided I didn't like the way I was living. Buying and selling businesses..."

"Well, it seems like we are getting off on the wrong foot," she interrupted. "Listen, I've got to get home, Dan. It's been a long day. I'm sure I'll see you soon if you're seriously buying the place next door." There was a disgusted tone to her voice. Dan reached down to give Freddie a little love before Kate turned and briskly walked away, mumbling to herself about the rotten luck, having him not only home, but next door to the studio. Blindsided, she hadn't seen that one coming.

Tugging on Freddie's leash to get back on their way, she immediately felt shame. She didn't have a right to interrogate him like that in their first meeting in years. She'd just been caught so off guard. She had never thought he'd come back. And buying the café next door. So much to take in after all this time. And why did he have to look so dang handsome? As she rounded the corner, she felt herself turn to take another look. No, Kate, she told herself. Turn around and keep walking.

And before she could take another breath, she ran into one of the guys she had briefly dated in the past.

"Brad, how are you?" she asked.

Brad was handsome with deep brown eyes, a quick smile, fun, flirtatious and definitely not the steady type Dan was.

"I'm good, Kate, you? Hey, Freddie, good boy."

"Me too. Just haven't run into you much."

"Probably because you don't hang out at the bowling alley or the pool table at Charlie's."

She laughed. "Yup. We never were a good fit, huh? I'm a homebody and you're, well, not."

"Nope. But always good to see you anyway. Take care."

It was always nice to see him too, and he made a good friend, just not the kind of good friend that could be her boyfriend. She started wondering why she had never met anyone as special as Dan in the decade since he left. Some of the guys she had dated had come close, but none ever measured up. He had set the bar high. That was true, but it was obvious to Kate that he no longer was the guy he was back then. He wouldn't have left her for so long if he was.

Chapter 3

As she and Freddie walked on, she found herself lost in thoughts of the past. A cool breeze gently blew across her face and hair. She smelled bonfires burning, enjoyed seeing the golden, red and orange maples, heard the sound of leaf blowers on the short walk home, crunched dried leaves underfoot. Just a few blocks from reaching her bungalow on Providence Lane, she stole a quick glance at Dan's childhood home on the corner of Oaks and Providence. Easily the stateliest house in town, the Tudor stood sentinel on the corner just a few blocks from the village. His dad still lived there.

Beacon was a quaint southern town located close enough to Charlotte, North Carolina, to almost be a suburb. Maybe as the big city spread towards them their borders would meet. Hopefully not any time soon though. Kate loved it just the way it was. The downtown area had over a century ago been laid out like a village. With a park like setting, leafy oaks and tall pines lined the walkways and lent their shade to picnic tables scattered throughout the square. Meandering walkways instead of the usual parallel downtown streets provided an atmosphere of days gone by. Businesses were housed in hundred years old and older brick store-fronts. Simpler times. The feeling often evoked was nostalgia, peace. Kate had never wanted to leave.

She had lifelong friends she could rely on. Her best friend Jenny had married her high school sweetheart Chris and they had two adorable little boys. Adam was four and Tyler, almost three. Shanti Bennett, Kate's other close friend still lived in Beacon but worked as a mortgage lender at one of the banks in Charlotte. She attended yoga classes when she could in the evenings so they saw each other frequently. Shanti hadn't dated anyone special yet either; she was Kate's usual sidekick. Andy and Amy were married now with one little girl five years old named Scarlet. They'd started dating each other in middle school. They had been young and carefree and it was all so simple back then. Kate had naively believed she and Dan could keep the magic. Well Amy and Andy had. So did Jenny and Chris. Two out of three wasn't bad, she supposed.

After all, she and Dan had been the couple everyone in high school had assumed would marry after college and live happily ever after with a passel of kids. But it wasn't meant to be. His career choice and move to the Big Apple had been a shock to her. Dan was laid back, fun loving, caring, and grounded. None of those attributes added up to his corporate choice of career. The only way she could begin to imagine why he had taken that route was that he was seeking his father's approval. And that didn't match up with who he was. She just couldn't fathom how he could be true to himself in that world. As she and Freddie walked on, her thoughts trailed deeper into the rabbit hole of how he could have changed so much. Years, it had taken her years to get over him. And then to have him show up again, out of the blue Carolina sky...

Ah, finally home. Other than the studio, there was nowhere Kate would rather be than her homey, welcoming bungalow. She especially loved the front porch and she could hardly wait until after Thanksgiving to don it with evergreen boughs and twinkling white lights. Every southern house needed a front porch in her opinion. She loved sitting on the porch swing with Freddie lying at her feet, reading for hours in the warm sun. Walking up the winding sidewalk past her rose bushes still blooming, the entire house greeted her like an old friend. As she opened the front door, she smelled the familiar scent of salted caramel. Her room fragrance made her at once feel at home and more than a little hungry.

She purchased the house five years ago once the studio became solvent, even profitable most months. She had decided back then that she and her mom spent enough time together at work, and she wanted a space to call her own. She found painting relaxing so the first thing she did was paint all the inside walls white, providing her with a blank slate to start decorating. Drawn to comfortable furnishings, she knew what she wanted when she saw it. Over the years she had slowly added one piece at a time, scouring antique malls, secondhand stores, and even yard sales. She had picked up her knack of putting it all together from her mom's decorating style and had created a home where her friends felt welcome and at ease.

After Kate fed Freddie and made sure his water bowl was full, she filled her clawfoot tub and soaked in lavender bath salts, sipping a mug of hot chocolate, her nighttime ritual of choice. She started reflecting on her childhood. An only child, she supposed that was why she was good at alone time. She liked being by herself. Treasured the quiet that kids with siblings probably didn't get as much. She often wondered if she was so close to her mom because Maggie usually had been her go to playmate as a kid. Without brothers or sisters to play with, she spent most of her free time with her mom through the years. That hadn't been so much the case with her dad. He had been more distant, busy at work. Most nights he didn't come home until after she was already in bed. Still, Kate always thought her parents had a storybook marriage. That bubble burst like an oozing over filled witch's caldron twelve years ago when Kate was a sophomore in high school and her dad's affair with a far younger woman came to light. He left town to start a new life and a second family. She saw him less and less over the years and was now down to hardly ever.

She had always struggled with the loss of her dad, but while she and her mom were at the yoga teacher training, about a month into it, they did an exercise that changed things for her forever. Since then, she had done the exercise too many times to count because it never seemed to fail her. They had all been asked to take out their notebooks and write a paragraph about something hard that they just couldn't get past. The biggest thing she was still dealing with at the time was her dad's decision to leave her and her mom just two years earlier. This is what she wrote:

'My dad left my mom and me two years ago to start a new family with a new wife and future kids of their own. I knew it must be my fault because my mom is wonderful, but I was a teenager with teenage troubles, and a teenage temper. I was too much for him so he left us. He didn't want me anymore and he didn't want to deal with an imperfect teenage daughter. I had probably never made him happy. It was all my fault and I can never fix it.'

The instructor asked them to then delete every single word that wasn't factual, that might just be them, making up stories that weren't even true, and then struggling to live with their version of what had happened.

Here's what she had left:

'My dad left my mom and me two years ago to start a new family with a new wife. I can never fix it.'

Wow. She had been taking the blame all along, stuck in her guilt, and none of what she believed was factual. She had made up a story. It made her miserable. But it was a story. A lie. Maybe she could never fix it. It wasn't even hers to fix. That had been a turning point for Kate.

Chapter 4

Startled back to the present time by the sound of Freddie boisterously greeting her mom, she realized she had been lost in thought so long that her bath water had grown almost cold.

"Be right down Mom!" she yelled downstairs. "Grab something to drink and get out the snacks if you don't mind." Quickly she toweled off, dressed in her most comfortable ratty old gray sweats and twisted her light brown hair into a ponytail. A natural beauty, like her mom Kate hardly ever wore makeup. A quick couple dabs of mascara and a little lip gloss was all she ever bothered with. Practicing yoga daily and running with Freddie kept her fit and she had always enjoyed her food. She believed firmly in her motto: Do what you need to do in order to feel the way you want to feel. Simple enough. At five feet tall and only one hundred ten pounds dripping wet, she was blessed with a fast metabolism and was built like a gymnast, but she didn't let her looks preoccupy her.

Joining her mom downstairs, she was glad to see that she had set out the sharp cheddar cheese and wheat crackers; Kate added a cluster of red grapes to enjoy as they sat down to plan the annual holiday party for Olde Beacon Village. Reminding Freddie to step away from their snacks, she turned to her mom, "Did you know Dan is back in town?"

"Dan? Your old Dan?" Her mom sounded surprised, and just a little too pleased for Kate's liking.

"The one and only. Dan Ivy."

"Wow, that's a bit of a shock. For a visit or for good? Gosh, he hasn't been back in years. Did something happen to his stodgy stingy old dad?"

"No such luck." Kate stifled a sheepish ugly laugh. "That was a terrible thing to say, huh?"

Her mom replied honestly, "Hon, it's hard to find the goodness in Harold Ivy. After June died, he dug even deeper into his drive for money. All he has ever cared about is buying and selling companies. More hasn't exactly made him any nicer. He's always in Charlotte now wrangling one deal after the other. He never lets anyone or anything get in his way of his pursuit of the almighty dollar. I've always been a little surprised that he even kept a house here, but enough about him. What did bring Dan back then, Thanksgiving?"

"You won't believe it mom." Kate munched on her cheese topped cracker.

"I guess he's buying the vacant café next door to the studio." She could hardly believe it herself.

"Whatever for? I thought he'd followed his dad's footsteps right up the corporate ladder."

"I did too. But I guess we'll find out soon enough. Remember, he is an incredible cook after all. Or at least he used to be. You know, Mom, ten years ago I thought he would do something like he's doing now. I knew he wanted to please his dad but I had no idea that he would go as far as he did in his attempt to win his dad's favor."

"Katie girl, back then I thought he would study business, find out what he wanted to do, and come back here. I have never seen high school kids so suited for each other. Your dad and I were high school sweethearts too, but looking back we really weren't a match for each other at all. Sometimes I think people end up together for the wrong reasons. Your dad and I sure did. We became a habit. And some habits are meant to be broken."

"Oh, mom, I wish you hadn't had your heart broken like that."

"Kate," she let out a loving sigh, "you are here because we got married. And so is the yoga studio. It's hard to deal with some mistakes. But that one blessed me with the best gifts of my life. Remember, it is true that the broken places in us are where the light gets in. Over the years light has been filling all the cracks of my broken heart. And I'm ready for the right kind of relationship now. But I know so much more about myself, who I am, and it would take a far different kind of man for me to fall in love again, someone I knew in my soul I could trust."

Chapter 5

Down the street, Dan stared at his dinner plate heaped high with his favorite meal. He loved to cook. At first, he taught himself so he and his dad wouldn't starve after his mom died. He'd only been twelve and his dad hadn't shown much interest in anything other than frozen meals and the occasional hamburger or tuna helper. He started making things like grilled cheese sandwiches and tomato soup. The first couple of years he just grilled white sandwich bread with a fake cheese and opened a can of soup. He laughed out loud at the memory of his first attempt. No butter on the bread and the stove flame set too high, he had created a burnt monster of a mess that not even their dog would eat. Eventually he started making homemade bread and experimenting with cheeses like gruyere, cheddar, provolone, and blue cheese. He slathered mayonnaise on the outside of the bread instead of butter. The difference was subtle and delicious. And he learned to make his soups from scratch.

Many of the recipes he would be offering at the restaurant came about that way, through experimentation. The roast beef and mashed potatoes and gravy started with white bread, deli roast beef and gravy from a jar. The potatoes came from a box. He had also worked on that over the years, learning to roast the beef and make the gravy from the drippings, experimenting until he had mashed potatoes that even had his dad raving. Dan eventually found it therapeutic. And he'd made his favorite tonight.

Pasta Bolognese. A tossed green salad. Cheesy bread. The kitchen smelled like an authentic Italian restaurant, like Riggio's in the village.

Still, he just couldn't muster his appetite. He had often wondered how it would feel when he saw Kate again. When they were standing there, face to face, she had knocked him for a loop. Even dressed in sweaty yoga gear she looked beautiful as ever. He always thought she was a natural beauty, had liked it that she was a pretty girl that didn't really seem to know it or care. Once they were standing there together, it felt like he was back in high school and the ten years hadn't passed. He knew he'd sounded defensive as they'd talked outside earlier and guessed that he felt like it was his fault they had drifted apart. Too caught up in college life at Duke and his career after, he hadn't put any energy into retaining what they'd had.

How had he become the man that he had fought so hard not to be, he wondered. As a kid he had resented his dad's love of business, putting it over everything else, especially him. It was complicated because underneath it all, Dan had wanted to please his father and live up to his expectations. Then he realized, he had become his father after all. Expectations and control. Without even consciously being aware, he had given his dad the control of his life, even into adulthood. It came down to that, he supposed. But the life Dan had carved out for himself was no fit at all for who he was at his core. He let out a deep sigh. How different his life would have been if his mom hadn't crossed the street just as the out-of-control truck careened around the corner.

Dan poured another glass of Cabernet and pushed back from the table. His dad would be home soon and maybe he'd be hungry. Dan wasn't sure how it would be to see his dad. Like every other time he had come home from New York and allowed himself to feel a little hopeful, he had set himself up to be disappointed, but he was still not able to keep that sliver of hope from working its way in.

Spreading out his plans for the café on the coffee table, Dan settled in front of the crackling fire to work out some of the details. His idea was to name it the Ivy Café. There were so many features about the place that were just right. He loved the windows on the street side where diners could watch outside for friends walking by, and hopefully passersby would find the inside view enticing enough to want to stop in for breakfast or lunch. The wall next to the yoga studio was old original red brick that he was grateful had never been painted. And the floor had been updated to a stained concrete. Not only were they on trend, but they would be easy to maintain. A large wall separating the front counter and glass fronted cases from the kitchen provided the perfect place to cover with chalkboard paint and write out menus seasonally. The chalkboard would be easy to change and it would also give him the opportunity to list soup of the day options. He would have to measure the space and play with laying out seating plans. All in good time, he supposed, but he was excited and felt real passion about his work for the first time in years.

Dan was glad the living room fireplace burned real wood. Sometimes it was a hassle but it lent a sense of coziness to the large room; the smell and crackle and colorful dancing flames was soothing. Looking down at the stack of papers he knew that he finally had found his passion and no matter how distracted he was, Dan could always focus on the café. For the first time in his professional life, he felt driven in an unforced way about his work. Dan knew he had just been robotically going through the motions for the past few years. Once the realization hit that he was living to work rather than working to live, he was beyond glad it hadn't taken him a lifetime to learn that lesson. Now his work would be a natural extension of who he was. He was pretty sure his dad would never understand. His father's priorities lined up with work and success coming in as number one, two, and three. Work was his life.

It occurred to Dan that he only had that single memory of a father focused on financial success. Even when Dan was little, his dad didn't play ball or help build model airplanes or read to him or participate in any of the other activities that his friends shared with their dads. Christmases after his mom was gone were never the same. He didn't even remember decorating a tree again. Before she died, he had wonderful memories of making cutout sugar cookies, dancing in the kitchen to holiday music, going to visit Santa at the mall. Since his mom was only in his life for twelve years, he was grateful that she was such a loving, doting mom. Not for the first time he wondered what a different life he would have if she were still here. Sadness covered him like an itchy wool blanket every single time he let himself go there. He tried to think of something good instead. Since she died, he had been advised to remember that happiness depends largely on what you choose to let into your thoughts. Basketball. Now that was a good thing to reflect upon.

Basketball was king in North Carolina. And Dan was one of thousands of boys growing up in small towns all over the state dreaming of playing one day for the Duke Blue Devils or the UNC Tar Heels. Duke was Dan's team. When he was eight years old the Blue Devils won the national championship, and again three years later when he was eleven. Really impressionable years for a kid that played every waking hour that he could. He had a hoop in his driveway and that's where he could be found until it was too dark to see the basketball or the hoop. He slept in his Blue Devil's jersey. His dad was atypical for a North Carolina dad in that he didn't play ball in the driveway with him and they didn't ever watch the games together. Luckily, Chris's dad ran the village general store but spent his free time volunteering to help coach the boys while they were in middle school. Dan was fairly tall as a kid and his buddy Chris was even taller. Chris's dad Rick was like a second father to Dan and a major influence. Dan worshipped him and probably any good qualities he developed could be traced to time spent with him. Sometimes it does take a village.

By the time the boys were in ninth grade, Dan was almost six feet tall and Chris was a couple inches over. They both made the varsity in their small town. By then Kate and Jenny were smitten with the boys. Like almost every other kid in their high school, they didn't miss a game. And they both had crushes on the star players. The feelings were reciprocated and the four of them became inseparable.

Dan's thoughts pivoted from his childhood memories to all the decisions he had made in the recent past. All the "what ifs." What if he hadn't lost contact with Kate after going to college? What if she had gone with him? Would she have ever gone to New York with him? Would he have come back to Beacon with her instead? Would they have married? Would they have kids by now? Would he never have met Belinda... gotten engaged to her?

Immersed in his thoughts and his plans for the café, he didn't hear his dad open the front door.

"Dan. What on earth?" Dressed for success in his custom fit suit, his greeting was more like a challenge. "Whatever are you doing here? And what's all this mess?" he demanded unkindly as he stood there like a cold cement statue in the doorway.

"Whatever am I doing in our home? Great to see you too Dad. I'm here for Thanksgiving. Thought it was time," he tried to keep the sarcasm out of his voice.

"Dan, I won't even be here Thursday. You did not even bother to call or text to find out. You just show up like this," his father rudely replied.

"I left you two voice messages, dad. And now you tell me you are going away for Thanksgiving. Really? I guess nothing should surprise me when it comes to you and business." He tried not to be surprised, but Harold was, after all his dad, and he couldn't help but hope sometimes.

"Yes. Duty calls. Problems in London. It is easier to get first class transatlantic flights on holidays."

"Well, ok then. I guess most people spend holidays with their families so there probably are empty seats." There. He'd let him have it, a little jolt of guilt thrown his way.

"So, Dan, what are you really here for? Big corporate buyout in Charlotte? Working with the banks..."

"Actually, Dad I have plans to..."

His dad's cell phone rang. "Have to take this." He charged up the stairs toward his den. Nothing shocked Dan about his dad anymore. But all the same, just another pang of disappointment.

RECIPES

Easy Creamy Pasta Bolognese Sauce to serve over your favorite pasta. We like spaghetti noodles.

- 3 T olive oil

- ½ yellow onion chopped

- 2 carrots chopped

- 3 stalks celery chopped

- 2 pounds ground beef or beyond beef

- 1 c good red wine that you would drink with dinner

- Large jar marinara sauce of your choice

- ½ c heavy cream or more to taste (I like it creamy)

- ½ c parmesan, more to sprinkle on top

Directions

- Sauté onion, carrots, celery in olive oil until slightly soft, about 5 minutes

- Add beef and cook until brown

- Stir in pasta sauce and wine and simmer about 15 minutes

- Add cream and parmesan until heated

- Serve over pasta with more parmesan

Cheesy Bread

- 8 oz mozzarella cheese

- 8 oz sharp cheddar cheese

- 2 T mayonnaise

- ½ c finely chopped green onion

- 1 clove minced garlic

- ½ t Italian seasoning

- ¾ stick butter almost melted

- One loaf of fresh Italian bread

Directions:

- Mix all ingredients and spread over bread that has been sliced in half lengthwise and placed crust side down on a foil lined baking sheet pan.

- Broil 3 to 5 minutes. Watch carefully.

- Cool a couple minutes before slicing with a pizza cutter.

Chapter 6

"**G**reat class, Maggie." Tammy was a tall wiry woman of fifty who could easily pass for forty. She was a regular in the six am class and was busy rolling up her mat to help clean the floor before leaving to begin her day job as the village florist.

"Thanks, Tammy. Always enjoy the energy you bring to class," Maggie smiled at her.

Tammy was more than a student. She had become a friend, always willing to step up and help out if they needed her. The studio was like a second home to Tammy. Fortunately, there were several students like her that felt more like family than clients. Kate and Freddie walked in and Tammy gave the dog his usual morning treat.

"Don't I know it," Kate joined the conversation, "Mom is the best and she always brings the fun, even early in the morning," she agreed with Tammy. "And Tammy, are you set to decorate Riggio's for the village party again this year?"

"Hold on a sec," Kate answered her cell. "Hey, Mom, Tammy, got to take this. It's Jenny. How could I forget that we were having coffee this morning?"

"Sorry Jenny. I can be there in ten," she promised, throwing her fleece coat back on and leaving Freddie to man the front desk. Kate reminded her mom to run a load of face cloths for her noon class and then rushed through the village towards the coffee shop. Charming, quaint, the businesses looked like they belonged in the pages of a storybook. She never took for granted the special place she got to call home. Why anyone would ever want to leave was beyond her imagination.

Kate hugged her oldest and best friend as soon as she arrived at the coffee shop where they met most Tuesday mornings. The aroma of coffee filled the room and if there was a better smell, Kate didn't know what it was. Growing up, it was always the first thing that woke her. She had to admit, the smell was even better than the taste. She smiled at her friend. If possible, Jenny hadn't aged a day in the ten years since they'd graduated. She still wore her straight blond hair long most days, put on a little more makeup than Kate, and dressed professionally for her job, but as soon as she got home, the makeup and suits were replaced with a clean face and sweats. Today she was dressed down with no appointments scheduled and looked relaxed in her black jeans and sunny yellow turtleneck, her long blond hair in a braid that almost reached her waist.

Chris and Jenny were easily two of the best people she knew. Jenny had become a successful realtor in town, and Chris ran his family's general store in the village. Jenny was her truest confidant and she was grateful for a friend she could rely on. As soon as they'd grabbed their hazelnut and vanilla coffees the two relaxed into easy chairs by the front window. After taking her first sip of coffee, Kate set it on the side table. Kate couldn't wait to tell Jenny about Dan's reappearance.

Jenny kicked off her boots and tucked her feet underneath her as she sat forward in the easy chair, blurting it all out before Kate could speak. One of her favorite things about Jenny was her forthrightness. There was never a speck of guile in her.

"I can't hold it in any longer. I've been sworn to realtor client privilege up till now, and I've just gotten the go ahead. You won't believe it." The words flew out in a torrent.

"Oh, I think I will. It's Dan, isn't it? He's buying the café." Kate let Jenny know she knew.

"Oh my gosh, how did you know? I felt awful keeping it from you," she frowned and leaned in toward Kate apologetically.

"I literally bumped into him last night when I was leaving to walk home from the studio."

"You don't know how much I wanted to tell you Kate. He just gave me the go ahead yesterday."

Kate hesitated. But only for a beat. "All forgiven. It's just so over-whelming. I always thought, back when we were together, that he'd follow his passion for cooking and maybe even head to culinary school. His dad had a stronger hold on him than I'd realized. Now here he is ten years later ready to come back home."

"Kate, I know, how was it seeing him? Any of the old feelings flood to the surface?"

"Oh Jenny. I don't know. I mean. We're different people now. I... Um, it's confusing me. So much to take in. I thought he'd left forever. You know that I was hurt for so long. And nobody I have dated has been right for me. Let's face it; I haven't really gone out much at all. Now and then I think about how my life is almost full. How many single guys have been hanging around town anyway?"

"I hear you, Kate, it's got to be hard. And maybe Dan is back for a reason, maybe not. But what about just taking it moment by moment, see what happens?"

Kate realized the subject was going to be a tough one for her. She needed to let it all marinate before she even talked to her best friend about him. "Let's change the subject. How are those little boys of yours? I still don't know what to get them for Christmas."

"Kate, Adam and Tyler have everything they need. I'm wishing I could give some of their toys away, not accumulate additional items, but I'm pretty sure they would have a different idea about that."

Jenny got a call from a client and Kate took it as a good time to get on with her day as well. Their conversation had brought back so many deeply buried memories of the four of them back in high school --- football games, dances, even just hanging out doing nothing together. Kate pushed those thoughts back where they belonged, gave Jenny a peck on the cheek and turned toward the door. And there was Dan coming through the entrance. Really? Was he going to turn up around every corner now? Beacon, North Carolina, was a town of just over five thousand residents and he was going to be next door to the studio. She realized the odds were good. Somehow, she was going to have to deal with it.

"Hi again," she managed, unable to meet his eyes. Weird running into him again after all those years apart. She felt deep down in her bones the rejection that had lived there since he hadn't returned home. That along with the wounds her father left by wanting a new family had kept her from completely moving on. She had been stuck, emotionally unable to settle into any lasting relationship. And so much of it was his fault.

Did she see the old twinkle in his eyes as he greeted her with his quick boyishly open smile in return? No. It had to be her imagination. They were finished. He was a different man than the boy she had loved. He'd turned that corner and had never looked back. Why did he have to come back here? All the old wounds were starting to fester again.

"Got to run," she mumbled and rushed through the door. She needed to teach her class at noon. That would take some major recentering with the unexpected and confusing emotions she could hardly set aside.

Kate walked by the hot dog stand as Billy Cooper was setting it up for the day. She waved at him and smelled the hot dogs; her mind flashed back to the ninth grade. Incredible the way aromas brought back memories. Jenny's family had moved from Asheville to Beacon over that summer.

She had left behind all her childhood friends and was ready to jump feet first into making friends in her new town.

Jenny had never been one to know a stranger so she invited all her homeroom classmates to come by her house for a picnic before the first fall football game. Her mom had stacked hot dog buns to the ceiling on top of the refrigerator, and her dad must have grilled enough hot dogs to feed the neighborhood; bags of potato chips spilled out on the kitchen counter.

Kate was the only one who showed up. She felt heartsick for Jenny; she almost cried. Jenny, on the other hand, laughed. She figured everyone had other plans and didn't take it personally for a second. Her brothers and sisters, mom and dad, and Kate became the party. By the time Kate and Jenny walked to the football stadium, their friendship was cemented.

Jenny's mom had frozen what was left of the food and pulled it out to reheat for the next party Jenny threw a couple of months later. The place was packed. As everyone got to know the new girl, they naturally gravitated to someone so fun and confident. To this day Kate and Jenny laughed about the party that wasn't, the night they became friends.

Kate sat down on a bench, reflecting on her decision to become a yoga teacher. Her mom had begun to take classes when Kate was in high school. Maggie had been devastated when her husband's affair came to light. Maggie's younger sister Ali, more like a best friend than a sibling, had been trying to get her to yoga classes in nearby Charlotte for years, but she'd always resisted, insisting that her daily walk around Beacon was the only exercise she needed or wanted. Maggie had been a young and fit forty-one. She'd only been twenty-five when Kate was born and even at sixteen, Kate had known she had lucked out in the mom department. Some of her friends clashed with their parents, even spoke terribly of them. Kate couldn't relate. They had their squabbles, but for the most part, she had an easy and open relationship with her own mom.

Well, she hadn't seen her dad's betrayal coming. And neither had Maggie. For the first time in Kate's life, she had seen her mom lost, depressed and withdrawn. She had felt powerless when she couldn't seem to help her mother. Once Kate's mom hesitantly started attending classes with her aunt, Kate began to see a shift in her. Slowly Maggie came alive again and Kate felt like she had her mom back. Kate would never forget the first yoga class she had taken as a junior in high school either. She had issues with her back even at a young age. The relief she felt was immediate. And her mom was starting to use the yoga tools she was learning to aid her already strong faith in beginning to heal emotionally from the devastating departure of her husband.

Back then it had been in the back of Kate's mind to maybe attend one of the colleges close to Duke to be near Dan, but mostly because he would be going to school there. She had no strong career urges of her own, except a deep desire to help others, so when her mom had announced her decision to begin teacher training in the fall following Kate's high school graduation, Kate shifted her plans to travel to California and take the course with her. It seemed like an opportunity of a lifetime and she could always start school the second semester. What Kate could not have realized at that tender age was the way that single decision helped to forge the future that she and her mom would carve out at their yoga studio.

Getting up off the bench, she was now ready to teach. She had needed that time to just sit alone, to spend time in quiet reflection. Now she could walk in and focus on her students, instead of on herself and her own worries. That was the best way to shift into the present anyway, to get interested in someone else and out of her own head. As she entered the studio, she inhaled the familiar scents of lemongrass essential oils that always relaxed her, ruffled Freddie's silky red fur, and walked into her noon class filled with friendly faces. Kate admired the aged brick walls, tall ceilings, and century old six feet tall windows with original windowpanes.

She took a deep breath and stood on the old oak floors, confidently ready to teach her class.

"Hi. Welcome everyone. So happy to be together today. Please come into child's pose."

Next door at the café, Dan was officially the new owner. He began to assess the space that would soon become the Ivy Café. Hoping for a soft opening on Christmas Eve, he knew he'd better buckle down and get to work. What a crazy thought that Kate would be next door after all these years. He tried without success to push the thought from his mind and to concentrate on the task at hand. His dad would be leaving for two weeks in London and he had to admit he was relieved that his father would be away. Theirs was a tense and strained relationship already and when Dan had told his father this morning about the café and that he had given up the corporate life, his dad had grown even colder. Enough time spent dwelling on that, he told himself.

Just then he heard the front door open and looked up in surprise to see Kate's mom peek in as she slowly entered the café. Growing up she'd felt like a bonus mom to him. Having lost his own mom at such a tender age, he had beyond appreciated her warmth and caring. They embraced and he felt a little of the safety he'd always felt with her maternal love.

"Dan, welcome home."

"Thanks, Mrs. Nola. It feels more like home now that I've seen you."

That didn't sound right to her ears. All Kate's friends called her Maggie now.

"Call me Maggie next time, okay?"

"I'll try," he told her, "so, what do you think? I'm finally going to do something I want. I have so many ideas for this place. I just don't even know where to start."

"What kind of café is it going to be?" she asked.

"I'm going for comfort food mostly. The kind of thing that might make customers want to become regulars, just good food cooked with the best ingredients. Mostly my old recipes and some we used to make at your house back in the day."

"I can't wait to become one of those regulars," she told him. "Planning to spend Thanksgiving with your dad then?"

"You may or may not find it hard to believe but my father won't be here for the holiday. Heading to London on business. Some things never change I guess."

"Please join Kate and me then," she spontaneously offered.

He happily, yet timidly accepted, not knowing how Kate would feel about it. Maggie wasn't so sure herself, but finding out that his dad was taking off for London on the holiday, she couldn't bear the thought of Dan spending Thanksgiving alone.

Once Maggie left the cafe, Dan thought about all that she had done for him after his mom died. Just a few years after his mom passed away, he started dating Kate and he practically moved into their house whenever he could hang out there. Maggie treated him special, and it was such a relief after his dad had stopped even feeble attempts at parenting. He helped cook meals in her kitchen and she in turn served as counselor, homework tutor, and a second mom to him. She was so nurturing toward their entire group of friends. Over the years he had met others who lost a parent young. Most of them had gone into counseling but his dad had never sought that kind of help for Dan. If it hadn't been for Maggie, he wasn't sure he would have adjusted as well as he had.

Kate didn't know it but Maggie had continued to give Dan birthday and Christmas presents over the years. When the kids were in high school, he didn't have his mom anymore, and for all practical purposes he didn't have his dad either. Maggie had become his maternal influence and she treated him as she would treat her own son. Once he left for college and then went to New York, she didn't want him to lose all sense of home. She kept him in mind and heart especially at the holidays. She always felt that Kate wouldn't really appreciate those gestures. Kate had, after all, felt like she had been abandoned twice, once by her dad, and once by Dan. But Maggie knew the goodness was inside Dan, and she wanted him to feel loved. Now that he was back, she hoped that Kate could see in him what she had always seen. He wasn't his dad. And he wasn't like hers either.

Chapter 7

After class, Kate walked out into the open air with Freddie in tow and felt the familiar appreciation she always had for North Carolina autumn temperatures. Of course, she loved watching romantic winter movies, enjoying the pristine snowy scenes, but she didn't have a desire to feel the cold. She appreciated the beauty, but as far as she was concerned the temperature didn't need to be any colder than it was right now.

A warm yoga studio was just right for her. Follow that up with a stroll around the village in moderate fall temperatures. Perfect. Well, almost perfect. She glanced into what was now Dan's café and couldn't help but notice her mom and Dan and the easy way they appeared to resume their friendship. She felt a pang of nervousness deep in her core as she didn't exactly feel the ease herself. She could never be an actress. When she felt uneasy, she couldn't fake confidence. She just couldn't. Just then Maggie walked out of the café.

"Hey Kate. I was just reconnecting with Dan." She looked uncomfortable. "I, um, I invited him to join us for Thanksgiving. His dad is going to London for work and..."

"Mom, you didn't!" Oh my gosh, running into him was one thing, but now she'd be spending the whole day with him. Her heart wasn't ready for that. Her pulse quickened. The ache in her heart was palpable.

"Mom, he betrayed me. I'm trying to get used to his coming back. I'll have to see him every day, everywhere I go, and now you invite him for Thanksgiving dinner?"

"Honey, he'd be alone otherwise. Ali and her family will be at Justin's parents this year so it'll just be the three of us. Maybe it will feel like old times."

"I seriously doubt that mom." But she reminded herself that Maggie was only doing what came naturally to her; she took a deep breath in, let a deep breath out, in an effort not to overreact. Thank God for yoga tools. She changed the subject.

"Mom, have you talked to Julie and Mike about the Christmas Eve party at Riggio's? Same time as usual?"

"I'm so grateful they always host. Yes, all set."

"Me too. I can't imagine it anyplace else, definitely the best place in town."

The Riggio's Italian Restaurant was the cornerstone of the village. Established in the century old stone landmark, the place had been there through three generations. The atmosphere was beyond remarkable, lots of stone and heavy woodwork, the place somehow felt cozy yet roomy. And the food was even better than the ambience. Kate would eat there every night if she could.

"Same time. Same place. Now let's get to Food Lion and grab the rest of our Turkey Day ingredients. I often wonder why we don't eat that meal more than once a year. Delicious!"

The single grocery store in town was packed, a small older market, nothing like the mega trendy stores popping up everywhere, they still always found everything they needed there. Shopping carts were bumper to bumper; they moved slowly through the aisles in Beacon's idea of a traffic jam, but it gave them a welcome opportunity to talk with neighbors, students, friends. She stopped to say hi to Judy at the deli and to Darla as she stocked shelves. And then, while looking at the bottom shelf in the veggie aisle for fried onions to top the green bean casserole, she turned to unexpectedly find Dan.

He seemed a little sheepish as he asked her if she was okay with her mom inviting him to join them for Thanksgiving dinner. "Do you want me to bring anything tomorrow?" he asked her.

"Any special ingredients you need for your hot chocolate. And yourself," Kate replied. "You'll deserve a break from your own cooking," a little laugh escaped in spite of her mood. "That didn't come out right. You know what I mean." He was an amazing cook.

"No offense taken. See you then," he said. "Have to get out of this crazy crowd."

Returning to her mom's house, Kate helped her with some advance meal prep and they decided to go out for dinner at Riggio's. The Wednesday night before Thanksgiving they always treated themselves to a pizza or a meal out. "Pizza or Riggio's?" her mom had asked.

"Riggio's for the win," Kate exclaimed, ready to sit down and enjoy a meal at her favorite restaurant. She was funny that way. Nothing, not even seeing Dan, ever put a damper on her appetite. She fit the old adage usually attributed to men. The way to this woman's heart was through her stomach.

As they waited for their server to take their order, they sipped Chianti and talked about the next day and made a plan for what to make when. The hardest thing about preparing the traditional holiday meal was that everything needed to be done the last twenty minutes, carving the turkey, whipping the potatoes, making the gravy, ...

"Mom, that guy over at the table by the far wall..."

"The one sitting alone, blue sweater, short gray hair, reading a book?"

"Yeah, that one. He took my yoga class Monday at noon. He's new to town. Seemed really nice. I kind of wonder what his story is."

"He's not bad looking," Maggie noticed aloud, subconsciously fixing her hair with her fingers and digging through her slouchy handbag for lipstick.

"Hmmm, you think so, huh," Kate ribbed her mom. She hadn't seen that look on her mom's face for a long time. And she had never heard her show interest in anyone since her dad left. Ever.

Kate gobbled a piece of garlic bread and brought up the elephant in the room, "I'm not sure it was a good idea to invite Dan, Mom."

Her mom looked lovingly into her daughter's beautiful hazel eyes. She knew Kate was having a hard time with it all.

"Oh honey, there's still so much magic between you two. Anyone could see it."

"I hate to say this to you, Mom, but if that's what you see, you definitely need to have your eyes examined."

Chapter 8

Freddie jumped up and started licking Kate's face to wake her up on Thanksgiving morning, his way of letting her know it was time to get up and go out for a run. She reluctantly left her warm bed, pulled on her gray sweats and long-sleeved tee from a 5K turkey trot six Thanksgivings ago, slipped into her well-worn running shoes, and grabbed his leash. Yoga and running were her tried and true methods of clearing her head, especially when there was as much on her mind as there was today; the more on her mind, the longer the run. Today was going to be a long one. One for the record books.

They hadn't made it very far when they ran into Amy and her daughter Scarlet, out for an early morning walk gathering leaves for their table. Kate gave Scarlet a hug and wished her a happy Thanksgiving as Freddie nudged lovingly but persistently into the little girl's hand until she softly petted him, dropping most of the leaves that she had picked up along the way.

Amy mentioned to Kate right away, "I heard Dan is back." She could always count on her friend to get right to the point. Kate replied that he sure was. She kept a straight face and didn't offer more.

"How are you doing with it?" Her old friend quizzed her gingerly, trying to keep the breeze from blowing unruly red curls into her eyes.

Kate laughed. "That's why I'm on this long run, trying to sort it all out. So many feels. Are you making the big meal for everyone today, Amy?" She changed the topic. Andy's whole family lived in town and Kate knew it would be a happy gathering.

"Jill and I are making it together, so it will be fun." Kate knew it would be for sure as Amy had a great relationship with Andy's mom.

"Well, I guess we had both better get going then. Mom invited Dan to ours, crazy huh?" She gave Scarlet a hug and picked up Freddie's leash.

Amy tried to hide a surprised expression. Good for Maggie, she thought, secretly hoping her two old friends would find their way back to each other.

After they had run about five more miles, Kate showered and dressed in her softest, comfiest gray sweater and favorite blue jeans. She was tempted to put on sweat pants knowing she would probably overindulge but wore the jeans as a nod to dressing up a bit for their guest. Before leaving, she took a second glance in the hallway mirror, went back to her bathroom and applied some mascara. She ran her hairbrush once more through her naturally wavy hair and left it down.

In half an hour she was in her mom's kitchen helping to ready the feast. "Freddie," she told her pooch, "Get back; go over to your bed. We don't need your help here." And before she could settle in, Dan arrived. He was too much of a cook to be left out of the meal preparations. Kate noticed his chestnut hair was receding just a bit. He looked a little more distinguished than he did when she saw him a few years ago. As the morning wore on, Kate made her best attempt to keep her distance from him. Physically she was in the room, but she didn't talk much, just tried to concentrate on the task of cooking. Emotionally she was close to her breaking point. Her heart was usually soft, but today it felt icicle cold and brittle enough to break all over her mom's kitchen floor. Yoga had taught Kate to be present in every situation, not always revisiting the past or reaching for the future, and she knew that truly was where the magic of life happened for her. Being present wasn't coming naturally today, however. Some things are easier said than done.

By early afternoon they sat down and enjoyed the dinner; thankfully, Maggie and Dan kept the dinner conversation light. Who had need for conversation with all the food they were feasting on anyway? Turkey, stuffing, the ubiquitous green bean casserole, mashed potatoes, candied sweet potatoes, cranberry relish, pumpkin pie...the deliciousness kept them stuffing their faces.

Maggie was interested in Dan's life in New York. She passed him the potatoes and asked, "Tell us about life in the big city."

Dan shrugged his shoulders, "It wasn't the way it is portrayed on tv and in the novels you read. It's hard to live there without millions of dollars, crowded, dirty, noisy..."

"But the theater, the restaurants," she prodded.

He replied gently, "That's the vacations people take there. Most of my friends and colleagues were dining on Chinese takeout and working around the clock to make it."

Kate couldn't help herself and belted out, "If you can make it there, you'll make it anywhere, it's up to you, New York..."

Dan laughed, "Yep. Pretty much."

As far as Kate and Maggie were concerned, the Christmas season commenced as soon as the Thanksgiving meal was over and decorating her mom's house was the plan for Thanksgiving evening. Tradition was important to them. They would be spending the rest of the day filling the house with holiday magic, starting with the Christmas tree.

Dan helped them wash and put away the dishes, then settled into the easy chair by the fire and fell asleep to the football game he was "watching" on tv. Kate and Maggie took the opportunity to go upstairs to the attic for the Christmas decorations. As Kate climbed to the top of the ladder to reach for a box of lights, she lost her footing; somehow, she managed to hand the lights to her mom successfully before falling off to the side and landing awkwardly on her ankle.

"Honey, are you okay? Gosh, here, let me help you up. Can you stand?"

"I'm, I'm not sure, Mom. I think it's twisted somehow. Ouch. Ooh. Yup. Something is not right."

By then Dan had made his way up to the attic right behind Freddie. He had awakened to the loud commotion, and got there as fast as he could.

"Oh, Kate, you okay? What happened?"

"I fell off the ladder. My ankle hurts a little. I can't really put any weight on it."

Maggie spoke up, "I think we need to get her to the doctor, but since it's Thanksgiving, maybe one of those 24-hour clinics?"

"Oh, c'mon guys, I'm fine. Please just help me get down the stairs."

The three of them carefully traversed the narrow, steep attic stairway one slow step at a time, not easy by any means but they eventually made it all the way to the first floor living room. And soon it became apparent that her ankle was swelling already and they did need to get her some medical attention. Maybe she was a bit vain after all. She was thinking more about being glad she had shaved her legs than she was about how swollen her ankle was. Reluctantly she agreed to go but only under the condition that she could stretch out in the backseat of Dan's car. An ambulance seemed over the top and way too dramatic to her. Maggie and Dan made sure she was comfortable and after they got her settled in, they arrived at the clinic within minutes.

Once Kate was ushered into the exam room, she looked up to greet the doctor. What a small world. Her new yoga student, the attractive new-comer they had spotted at Riggio's last night was her attending physician. He welcomed Kate with an extended hand, introduced himself as Dr. Smith, and they immediately laughed as the two recognized each other. "Call me Jack," he suggested, "since you are after all, my yoga teacher." Kate agreed and just happened on purpose to notice that he wasn't wearing a wedding ring.

Once her ankle was examined and X-rayed, Jack gave them the good news that it was only a sprain and nothing was broken. She would need to rest, ice it, and take some pain relievers every four to six hours. He wrapped it in an elastic bandage to keep the swelling down.

"How long will it take to heal?" Kate wanted to know.

"The good news is you'll be back on your feet before Christmas, only a week to three weeks if you follow the protocol I just outlined. And I'm sure you want to teach tomorrow, but take it easy, okay?"

"Oh, and we will make sure she does," her mom replied and Dan nodded in agreement.

As they got back into the car Maggie turned to see that Kate was comfortable and was surprised to see the smile spreading across her daughter's face.

"Well, that's a big smile. You must be relieved that it's only a sprain."

"I am, Mom, but the smile is for a different reason. And you know it. I guess we know what the handsome guy from my class is doing in town."

Her mom couldn't help but return the smile. "I guess we do."

"He wasn't wearing a wedding ring, Mom."

Maggie left that one hanging in the air.

Returning home, Maggie carved out a comfortable spot for Kate on the couch. Freddie carefully lay down beside her and plopped his head on her stomach for consolation. The sweet dog had been her constant companion for the past four years and he always instinctively seemed to know how to show her he cared. Dan brought out a bag of likely expired frozen peas from the freezer to start icing her ankle, then he went upstairs to bring down the Christmas décor. Kate felt bad that she couldn't help decorate, but she did enjoy the Mexican cinnamon spiced hot chocolate Dan prepared.

"Thanks, Dan. I have to admit that you make the best hot chocolate. Would you believe just the other day I grabbed the cumin instead of the cinnamon, and shook in a little more than I had meant to anyway?" She laughed. "Cumin is definitely not the right spice for hot chocolate."

"Did you drink it?" Dan looked at her skeptically.

"Sure did. I added a healthy dose of peppermint mocha creamer to the mug and drank it anyway. From now on I am going to read the spice jar label."

Kate sat back and in spite of herself enjoyed sipping the hot chocolate as she watched her mom and Dan decorate the tree. A short week ago if someone had told her this is how her Thanksgiving would shake out, she would have laughed in disbelief.

Chapter 9

Friday morning the yoga studio was filled to the brim for their annual two-hour long turkey burn. It was one of Kate's favorite classes of the year. Every student who stayed in town for Thanksgiving seemed to attend; she and her mom co-taught it. She settled into the makeshift chair and propped her foot on a second chair topped with a pillow. Kate began the class by asking everyone to take the little piece of paper they had picked up as they entered the studio, and to write one thing they were grateful for that they could use as an intention as they practiced.

She tossed out suggestions, "You might choose gratitude, love, joy, presence, or anything else you need more of in your life." Then she asked them to take a comfortable seat, close their eyes, and take three deep inhales and exhales. She surveyed the class, making sure to take note of every student. Scanning the third row, she spotted a new student. It was Dan. She had to admit it took courage to take a two-hour turkey burn for his first class. Yet there he was. What would possibly prompt him to take their turkey burn, she wondered as she struggled to teach her part of the class without staring at him. But when she did look at him, it was obvious to her that he had never taken a yoga class before. Oh wow, she also noticed handsome doctor Jack Smith in the back row. She took a deep breath and focused on teaching the whole group, not singling out those two.

After class she asked Dan what he thought of it.

"It's my first class. Probably obvious," he laughed, "I know I am a disaster at this, but I sure liked the nap at the end of class, especially the cold eye cloth." He was surprised at the relaxed way he felt once the challenging class was over and wanted to book another ten classes to help him navigate the stress of the next month's café readying project. She was glad he enjoyed it, but hoped that maybe he would take her mom's or one of the other teachers' classes and she could avoid teaching him. Dan interrupted her thoughts and mentioned his plan to deep clean the café that afternoon.

"I wish I could be of help," she told him more out of politeness than any real intention, "but with this ankle…"

Jack was nearby digging out his shoes and coat from one of the cubbies, and chimed in. "Sorry to butt in, but I couldn't help overhearing. You did an excellent job of propping up your ankle so that you could teach, but no manual labor today."

Kate had to agree with Dr. Smith. She also couldn't help but notice that before he left, he had stopped by the counter and he and her mom were chatting easily.

So, he had at least taken two classes this week and the fact that he took the two-hour long class probably meant that he already practiced yoga. Good sign. He and Maggie just looked like they were hitting it off.

Dan asked, a little awkwardly she thought, if he could make dinner for her tonight.

"After you deep clean the café alone? No way."

"Making dinner isn't work for me, Kate. It's my way of relaxing. Honest."

She hesitated. Everything was happening too fast for her, but she reluctantly agreed. "Ok then, a girl has to eat." He was a good cook and she accepted in spite of her concerns about spending time alone with him. Did she hurt her good sense along with her ankle when she fell? She couldn't help but giggle about the possibility as she agreed to join him for dinner.

"Pick you up at six," he smiled and left it at that.

Later as they made it back to his childhood home, he helped her to the couch where it would be easy for her to eat at the coffee table and still prop up her foot.

"What's cooking?" She needn't have asked. That amazing aroma. Whoa. She knew that tasty smell. "You remembered. My favorite." She felt a flush fill her cheeks at the thought of the sweet gesture he had taken, not only to cook for her, but to remember the comfort food she loved.

"I sure did. Shepherd's pie. You always went for comfort food like macaroni and cheese or Shepherd's pie."

"That I did. Still do. Smells delicious. Let me guess. In that case, you are planning on apple crisp for dessert, your mom's old recipe."

"We shall see. Got to keep some surprises up my sleeve." It had been a long day for him working at the café, but being with her again was energizing him. He decided to up the festivity level.

"Glass of Sauvignon Blanc?"

"Don't mind if I do. Thanks." Why did he invite her over and even more curiously, why did he remember to make her favorite? She couldn't help but ponder, but she reminded herself that she needed to be on guard and take things slowly.

They both seemed to enjoy dinner and the quiet company of old friends sitting comfortably with each other; at least it felt that way to Kate. She had to admit it surprised her how easily she could relax into his company after all this time, especially since she was trying so hard to protect her heart.

"That was delicious." She smelled the cinnamon sugary goodness of the apple crisp and could hardly wait until it melted in her mouth. "And I guessed right on dessert. So there you go. Speaking of which, sorry to literally eat and run, but I've got to go home and get to bed after dessert. I'm teaching the six am tomorrow."

"I'll drive you home after dessert then. I kind of like it that you are dependent on me," he admitted. Hearing that, she resolved right then and there not to stay reliant on him. Tomorrow she would find something to help her get around on her own. This was just one fluke, one meal. That's all it was. Why would she let herself think otherwise?

Once they reached her house they lingered for a while in his car, once again chatting like the old friends they had been. How conflicted could her feelings get, she kept thinking. Her thoughts were interrupted as Dan wrapped her up in a bear hug, helped her into the house, said goodnight and turned to head for home, happier than he'd been in a long time. Freddie was at the door, ready for his nightly walk; Dan noticed Kate sigh with regret that she couldn't take him.

"You know I've always loved dogs, Kate. He's got to go out for a walk. I'll take him, at least around the block."

Kate wasn't about to turn him down. Once Freddie heard the word 'walk,' it was a done deal anyway.

"Thanks again, I guess. Really appreciate it." She was grateful, she had to admit.

Dan had enjoyed walking Freddie. It actually turned into a far longer walk than he had planned and he always did his best thinking on a good walk or run. After Dan returned the pup to Kate, he found a second wind and had so many ideas swirling in his head that he took a quick shower and sat down to finalize his winter menu. The café would be open soon enough. At least a soft opening by Christmas Eve. He'd start with breakfast and lunch, maybe keep the hours seven am to three pm Monday through Saturday.

After a couple hours he'd sketched out a rough menu.

Breakfast:

Coffee, tea, milk, hot chocolate, orange juice, cranberry juice

Homemade cranberry walnut granola

Pancakes of course. Several options

Bacon and sausage links

French toast

Eggs. Every which way

Home fries

Grits

Biscuits and gravy

My specialties of Eggs Benedict and western omelets

Vegetarian options as well

That was a good start for breakfast. He'd keep it simple and high quality. Take it from there, maybe bring in some pastries from the bakery a couple blocks away. Especially the sourdough cinnamon buns and Danish pastries filled with cream cheese and blackberries

Lunch:

Same beverages. Also, sodas and sparkling water.

Hot turkey or roast beef sandwiches

Cobb salad

Hamburgers/beyond beef burgers with French fries

Cheese plates with fresh fruit

Grilled cheese and tomato soup

Green pepper honey mustard and cheddar cheese on a bagel

Daily soup specials

Desserts:

Texas sheet cake, seasonal pies, homemade ice cream

Way past midnight he fell into a deep sleep and slept better than he had in a long while.

He made a western omelet for breakfast and reminisced about the great time he'd had with Kate last night. Why hadn't he seen what they had years ago? Could it work now? He was starting to hope so, but he was pretty sure that she wasn't on the same page. Heck, they might not even be reading the same book.

That morning Maggie drove Kate back to the clinic so she could pick up an air cast to stabilize her ankle and she wouldn't have to be ferried around anymore as it healed. She had become independent over the past few years and wasn't in the mood to start leaning on anyone now. And she was definitely not the least bit interested in relying on Dan Ivy. That dinner last night was nice, but it was a one off.

Dr. Smith came out into the lobby as they were making the purchase. What a common name. Kate wondered why she hadn't recalled it. But it seemed that her mom was already on a first name basis anyway. Kate also noticed that her mom had paid a little more attention to her appearance today. She was wearing a chocolate brown sweater that drew attention to her almond shaped deep brown eyes, highlighted today with plum eyeliner and a lightly shimmery eye shadow.

"Jack, it was great seeing you at the six o'clock class this morning," Maggie offered.

"I find it is the best time of day for me to practice." He told her that if he started the day with yoga, he felt like he could concentrate on his work better. "And you teach a great class."

Kate was glad her mom taught that class. Noting the smile on her mom's face, she hoped Jack Smith would take the class every morning.

She couldn't take Freddie on his morning runs or nighttime walks, but Dan had enjoyed it so much the night before that they worked out a schedule for Dan to take him.

He promised that it would be as good a deal for him as it was for Freddie. He needed the exercise and it was refreshing to be back in their small town where it felt safe to be out at night and he could look up and actually see the stars.

RECIPES

Shepherd's pie

- Preheat oven to 350 degrees

- Grease a 9 by 13 glass oven dish

- 3 T olive oil

- Medium yellow onion chopped

- 2 carrots chopped

- 2 stalks celery chopped

- 1 garlic clove minced

- 1 ½ pounds ground beef or beyond beef

- 8 oz can tomato sauce

- 1 T Worcestershire sauce

- 6 large potatoes, cut into 1inch pieces

- ¼ c milk of choice

- ½ stick butter

- 8 oz sharp cheddar cheese

Directions:

- Sauté vegetables in olive oil about 5 minutes

- Add garlic for one minute

- Brown beef

- Add both sauces and stir in for a couple of minutes

- Boil potatoes at the same time in salted water until tender

- Drain and mash potatoes with milk and butter

- Spread beef mixture in glass oven dish, top with mashed potatoes, and cook in oven 25 minutes

- Add cheese for 5 to 10 minutes or until melted

- And enjoy!

Homemade cranberry granola (we eat this almost every day at our house)

- Preheat oven to 350 degrees.

- Layer aluminum foil over a large sheet pan, hopefully with edges.

- In a large bowl stir together

- ½ cup melted coconut oil

- ¼ cup packed brown sugar

- ¼ cup organic maple syrup.

- Add a tsp of sea salt

- 1 Tbsp of vanilla

- 2 Tbsp of pumpkin pie or cinnamon spice

- Stir well.

- Add 4 cups of old-fashioned rolled oats

- 1 cup chopped walnuts, almonds, or pecans.

- Stir and pack onto prepared sheet pan.

- Bake 11 minutes. Gently stir the mixture and pat it down.

- Bake 11 minutes more.

- Allow to cool on the counter and add 1 cup of dried cranberries.

- Store in a tin.

- We enjoy it with almond milk and sometimes sliced bananas.

I make it without nuts or dried cranberries for my three-year-old grandson. He loves it.

Apple crisp

- Preheat oven to 375 degrees

- Grease a 9 by 9 baking dish

- Choose sweet and tart apples, peel and slice enough to fill the dish at least a couple of inches

- Lightly sprinkle lemon juice over them and stir right in the baking dish

- Make mixture of

- One stick butter, crumbled into balls with fork

- 2 T cinnamon

- ¼ c cane sugar

- ¼ c packed brown sugar

- 1 c white flour

- And cover apples with mixture

- Bake uncovered 30 to 40 minutes.

We like vanilla ice cream served on it while hot.

Chapter 10

Christmas tree lighting in the village square was always held the Sunday following Thanksgiving. The sky overhead was a clear Carolina blue and it was chilly enough for Kate to wear her red bulky cable knit Christmas sweater, green stocking hat, and matching scarf. On her way over, Kate drove by kids out playing ball in driveways and riding bikes along the sidewalks. She would have rather been walking, but decided to drive and baby her ankle. Kate loved the tree lighting, and thankfully wasn't in charge. All the village businesses took turns and this year it was the general store's turn so the Spring family was coordinating the event. Soon it would be dark and the tree would light up the village square.

They'd convinced Dan to set up a booth with his homemade hot chocolate and several of the businesses donated Christmas cookies. The general store provided an assortment of their old-fashioned fudge. Always a fun family event, most everyone in town came out and it was considered the official start of the season. Positioning herself at the front, close to the tree, she turned to see Dan come up beside her, wearing an old Beacon high sweatshirt and ballcap.

"I see you picked up a boot. Is it okay to walk on it now, then?" he asked.

"I'm managing fine. Seems like you are popping up everywhere I go. What's with that, anyway? You are confusing me. You were gone for so long and now you just act like nothing happened. Like all the years didn't go by at all."

He was taken aback by the chill of her words and couldn't help but defend himself. "I tried to tell you the other day. I guess you don't think it's possible to change. But I have. It feels so good to be back in town. And at Christmastime," he rambled on. "I roughed out a trial menu for the café the other night. Your favorite bagel sandwich made the cut. I make the bagels from scratch, and if I say so myself, they're good."

She remembered back in high school when lunch funds were low, she'd found a way to add a veggie and cheese to her bagel order and it would still be a bargain. Slathered with honey mustard, and piled high with green peppers and sharp cheddar, she had eaten it almost every day.

"I'm happy with my winter menu," he went on, "but I am definitely going to need to hire some help if I want to serve it all. Hope I can find someone soon."

"I overreacted, Dan, and I'm sorry I was so harsh. I just feel so confused right now," Kate relented and went on to say---interrupted by the tree lighting countdown:

5 ,4 ,3 ,2 ,1...They joined the familiar cheer. "Merry Christmas!"

The tree was lit. Spectacular as always.

A crowd was beginning to swarm around Chris and Jenny.

"Great job guys! Hey Chris, good to see you man. It's been too long. Wow you little guys are growing up fast." Dan high fived the boys.

Jenny and Kate trailed Adam and Tyler as the boys ran to the cookie table.

Chris and Dan had a chance to sit on a nearby bench and catch up. Chris tilted his head toward Kate. "How's it to be back, buddy?"

"Pretty good man. Really good." And he meant it, but he didn't think Kate felt the same. Not at all. Just then the gals returned with the Spring boys. Dan was elated to be back and to be experiencing once again the official first Beacon holiday event.

Just then they smelled smoke, heard fire trucks, at first in the distance, then closer, now too close. Something in the village was on fire. The assembled group headed toward the sirens that were blaring terribly, way too close. Reaching the fire, seeing and smelling the heavy black smoke fill the sky, they watched in disbelief realizing that it was Riggio's ablaze; thankfully no one was inside. They were mercifully closed for the Christmas tree lighting. The festive evening mood turned somber as those gathered began to take in the destruction. The loss of a landmark, even more devastating, the loss of their beloved friends' restaurant. Their only immediate consolation, no one had been hurt. Out of the corner of her eye, Kate spotted Jack Smith practically rushing into the restaurant to make sure no one was injured. The firefighters had to pull him back and assure him that the place was empty. Kate joined the stunned group of those who were closest in relationship with Julie and Mike as they surrounded them with loving hugs. Helplessness hung heavy in the night air.

The Springs, Maggie, Kate, Dan, along with countless other families stood by wishing with their hearts and souls they could do something to fix it, knowing they couldn't.

As the firefighters began to talk with the Riggio's, the group gathered back at the Christmas tree. Kate noticed her mom chatting with Jack, but didn't feel like staying around to ask her about him. Quietly and somberly, everyone made their way home. The acrid smell of smoke lingered in Kate's nose for hours.

No one slept well that night in their small town. Word quickly spread Monday morning that there would be a meeting at the community center that evening to brainstorm fundraising ideas in order to support the restaurant in any way they could. One wonderful thing about a small town is the way everyone comes together when one of their own is in need.

Kate's Aunt Ali spearheaded the effort. She'd grown up with Julie Riggio.

Their bond was a tight one so that, and the fact that she had the biggest heart of anyone Kate knew, made her the natural leader. She stood at the podium in front of the packed room, barely peering over the top; Kate inherited her short stature from her aunt. Ali had the sinewy figure of a runner who never sat down. Her long curly dark blond hair had a mind of its own and tumbled past her shoulders as she stood there in a typical Ali style of clothing all her own, a mix of easy flowing pieces that somehow always worked on her. Ali's broad shouldered ruggedly handsome husband Justin stood at the white board, recording every idea. His large physique was only outmatched by his heart. Both school teachers, they represented to Kate the best of humanity. As the whiteboard filled with suggestions, the group decided to focus on three:

Every business could donate five percent of December profits.

Rebuilding efforts would begin ASAP.

There would be a month-long giftwrapping fundraiser.

Finally, someone asked the other question on everyone's mind.

Where would they hold the annual Christmas Eve party?

Dan wanted to offer the café, but it wasn't nearly big enough. Kate agreed, but what if they utilized the yoga studio also? The crowd could easily flow between the two establishments. Great idea. It was decided. But how would the café ever be ready in time? This was a far bigger goal than a soft opening. The great thing about a small town once again came to light. Kate and Dan had at least twenty close friends from high school still in town. Together they would find a way. Three weeks to go. Time to spring into action. Starting tomorrow. But that was going to mean spending so much more time with him. She was beginning to wonder just a little bit if he was telling her the truth. Could he have changed?

Why was he back, really?

Ali and Kate sat at a table alone at the end of the evening. Justin and Ali had driven separately so he went home to see that their adolescent boys finished their homework and got to bed at a decent time. The two women had always been close since Ali had all boys and Kate was Ali's only niece. It was almost like having a daughter of her own, but as her aunt, Ali could take off her parenting hat and just love her. Kate felt like she could tell her anything and had confided in her plenty of times over the years.

Aunt Ali tiptoed into the water, her hazel eyes gazing as if in a mirror at her niece's, "How's it going with Dan since he's been back, Kate? He was gone a long time but I never got the impression you had those strong feelings for anyone else."

"He did set the bar pretty high Aunt Ali. The guys I've dated over the years never really measured up to him. Even in high school he had that special something that made him seem more mature than his years."

"Oh, honey I could always see that when I spent time with you two. Even through the rough times after your dad left, he was there for you and your mom."

"I think he needed mom too after losing his own. And in a way I think mom needed him. It gave her two of us to love and dote on. No one else has ever come close for me, but he was in at least one deep relationship. I heard through the grapevine that he was engaged for a while. We never have talked about it. And he hasn't brought her up."

"Do you want to know more Kate? If you're falling for him again, maybe it's time to talk about it."

"Oh, Aunt Ali, I'm determined not to fall for him again. I don't want to give him an opportunity to break my heart one more time. We aren't the same people as the kids we were back then. Everything is still so new. And yet with our history it doesn't feel like new as much as ... I don't know," she shook her head.

"Comfortable. Right? Even meant to be? Determination will only get you so far where love is concerned. I'm afraid love wins over determination, sweet girl."

"I'm starting to think so." What? No. Where did that come from? Her Aunt Ali had a way of understanding her. She always had. Kate would not fall for him again.

"By the way, has mom mentioned anything to you about our new yoga student, Jack Smith?"

"Maybe she has. Maybe she hasn't," her aunt laughed. If I told you, I'd have to kill you."

Kate returned the laugh. She respected her aunt's loyalty to her mom, but she sure was curious.

"Hey, looks like we'd better close this place and call it a night. I didn't realize everyone else had left." They threw away their empty cups and straightened out the chairs. Turning out the lights, and locking the door, Ali hugged her as Kate told her aunt she loved her.

"Love you more Katie girl." That old nickname her mom and aunt still called her now and then made her feel so good.

Five years younger than Maggie, Ali was only twenty when Kate was born and she didn't get married for another eight years so she helped raise her, in all the fun ways. Kate remembered Ali being the one who took her to Claire's for her ear-piercing milestone when Kate was only twelve. She still didn't know if her mom had given the okay beforehand or not. Afterwards, to mark the occasion, she took her out and let her pick out a new outfit. By then Ali was pregnant with Kate's first little boy cousin, who would eventually become the oldest of four. Kate was old enough for them to feel more like nephews than cousins. She doted on them like Ali had always indulged her.

Kate had countless memories of fun with Aunt Ali, one of the best being that every time she wanted to spend the night with her aunt as a little girl, the answer was always yes. One year when she was four years old, they got out sleeping bags and slept all night under the Christmas tree. They didn't miss a year after that until Ali's first son Cheydon was born.

From the time Cheydon was four, Kate returned the favor, and he was now sixteen. He slept under the Christmas tree once a year at her house until he was twelve. She thought he might miss it now, but he was too old and cool to admit it if he did. She still kept the tradition going with Declan, now twelve. Everett had "graduated out of the experience" two years ago.

Griffin was only ten so at least she had two more years of the Christmas sleepovers with him. Such great family traditions. She fell asleep smiling at the memories. As Kate lay her head on her comfy cotton pillowcase that night and pulled up her fluffy down white comforter, she fell into a restful sleep. Talking with Aunt Ali had unburdened her in a way she had not even realized she needed.

The next morning found everyone who had been at the community center trying to figure out how they could best help Dan get the café up and running in time to host the Christmas Eve party. Their hearts were heavy for Julie and Mike and their employees who were all trying to come to terms with what didn't yet feel at all like a new normal. If anything, all Julie's years of yoga practice were reminding her that staying in the present moment was the only way to find any peace at all. Thoughts of the past would bring grief and the future, anxiety. What could she do in the present, she wondered? Mike was having those same thoughts but more along the lines of his fallback in hard times; getting his mind and actions off himself and serving others was the only was he knew to not feel paralyzed in fear this morning.

They talked it over and came to the same conclusion. Dan had mentioned that he had no cooks or waitstaff lined up yet. That was a way to help him and at least some of their beloved staff. The cooks and waitstaff, if they wanted, could pitch in at the future Ivy Café. The twosome headed to the café to talk with Dan who had arrived early that morning himself, not sure what his first step should be.

Hugs were the only greeting they needed upon arriving at the café. Dan asked them if there was any indication of how the fire started. Mike told him that the fire department chief said it was usually a faulty heating system in cases like this and that there would be further investigation. Then he told Dan the reason they were there. Tears leaked out of their eyes and Dan's as they shared their idea with him. "Gosh, if your employees are interested, it sounds like it could be a temporary help to all of us," Dan managed.

"Amen to that," the Riggio's agreed. They were the definition of people who are salt of the earth. Good, hardworking, and hard to keep down, even on a day like this.

"Now what can we do to help?" They managed a chuckle. "We are pretty familiar with this business."

Dan remarked, "That might be the understatement of the year." The three of them rolled up their sleeves and got started.

Next door Kate and Maggie sat cross legged on gray bolsters stacked on the hardwood floor of the studio, Freddie sprawled out between them. They began talking about the logistics of having the party at both the yoga studio and the café. Maggie raised the question of how they would decorate.

"How about a green and white theme, mom? Ivy, to honor the café, and white, well, just because it would create a winter wonderland feel."

"Great idea, let's call over to the flower shop, talk to Tammy, and see what she thinks so we can finalize the decorations at least."

Tammy was excited to help and had some great ideas about white candles and mason jars to mix with the ivy, the more lights the better.

The two women were tackling the topic of fixing the menu with the caterers when Dan joined them in the yoga studio. Kate was reminiscing about how nice it was when Riggio's hosted. The food was delicious every time and it hadn't occurred to her until now how much she took it for granted. She said as much.

"I can handle the food," Dan offered. "I am opening a café after all."

Kate and Maggie didn't want him to have to. They were thinking how nice it would be for him to enjoy the party. "No pun intended," Kate said, "but you have enough on your plate this month." They made the decision to go with the caterers.

Meanwhile Chris had figured out a way he could help get the café up and running and went over to see Dan to share his idea.

"Hey man, how's it going?"

"You wouldn't believe it, Chris, the Riggio's were here offering to help out by lending their employees. Seems like a win /win for the time being. I can hardly believe that they could come

He shook his head in amazement.

Not missing the longing look he saw on Dan's face, he jabbed him with his elbow.

"Good things brewing?"

"Starting to percolate."

"You know she's really never had a serious relationship since you two. Not to stick my nose in where it doesn't belong, but...have you, um talked any about your engagement with Belinda?"

"Nah. I haven't. It's over so I don't see any reason. Except."

"What?"

"I guess it's not as over for Belinda as it is for me. She's called a couple times. Left messages. I haven't called her back."

"Hmm. I think if I know women, at least the way I know Jenny, Kate would probably want to know. Think about it. Anyway, I came over to run an idea by you. What if I scour flea markets, antique stores, resale shops, friends' basements and get an assortment of kitchen tables and chairs for the cafe, would that help out?"

"Oh man that would be awesome. You sure you've got time? Whatever it costs, I'll pay, and more."

"Got the time. And I'll enjoy it. We will figure out the payment later. Done."

Good things seem to always come in threes. First the kitchen help, now the tables, and then Maggie stopped by next to offer help getting ahold of Dan's food vendors and ordering his list of ingredients. She loved the idea of taking a break from the studio and getting her hands on a new project. All these incredible old friends gave Dan the opportunity to line up some new kitchen equipment and paint the chalkboard lining the back wall, which allowed him to write out the winter menu. He stood back and admired his handiwork. Looked good.

None of this would have happened in New York. Sure, small towns have reputations for being places where everyone knows what everyone else is doing, who they're seeing, even thinking they know all the details of their personal lives. But there was an upside too, and he was glad. Friends were coming out of the woodwork with ways to help him. Having lived the past few years where it felt like it was all up to him, like the world was sitting heavy on his shoulders, he was grateful once again for this small town.

Winter Stroll was slated for this Friday night. He decided he would open his doors for hot chocolate flights. That would be his way of donating profits to the Riggio's. After all the goodwill pouring his way, he could send some in their direction. Winter Stroll was a town favorite. Coming in on the heels of the Christmas tree lighting, the village swelled with Beacon citizens as well as those from neighboring towns. Christmas carolers, dressed as they would have a century ago, sang on the bookstore corner. The coffee shop offered Christmassy dessert-like hot mugs of heaven. Every shop in the village provided holiday treats, and shoppers got a chance to finalize their purchases. This year the community center would be staffed with volunteers wrapping gifts so all donations could go to supporting Riggio's rebuilding efforts. The true meaning of Christmas was filling the air.

And now Dan's thoughts returned again to Kate. He couldn't believe he'd ever fallen for Belinda. She stood for everything his corporate life represented. And none of it was the real him. A part of him had been missing and the puzzle pieces were starting to fit easily in place again. Dan had a theory that life was a lot like putting a puzzle together. Once the edges were assembled, the rest of the pieces were still a scattered mess. Some days it was hard to put even ten pieces in, but one day the puzzle began to take shape and they easily fit. The picture became clearer and clearer.

The edges of his new life had come together to form the border and the pieces were starting to create a new beautiful picture. Come to think of it, that'd be a fun way to get to know each other better again. He could invite Kate to spend some evenings assembling a holiday puzzle while they taste tested recipes for the café. He would ask her tonight at the Spring's ugly sweater party if she'd like that.

Chapter 11

Kate was upstairs at home dragging down her ugliest Christmas sweater from the top closet shelf for the party tonight. Her mind drifted away from the annual party Jenny and Chris threw each year. She remembered when she and Maggie were looking through old family photo albums last week and she had remarked to her mom about the ugly sweater cookie exchange her mom used to host when Kate was a little girl. Maggie, Aunt Ali, and at least fifteen of her mom's friends were all wearing prize winning ugly sweaters and Kate had said as much. When her mom could finally quit laughing, she managed to inform her daughter that those had been fashionable sweaters; they wore them as many days as they could in November and December. Now they were designated as ugly. And Maggie had to admit, it was a funnier twist. Kate laughed as she buttoned up her most hideous Christmas green sweater with a brown Rudolph and his battery- operated blinking red nose. She completed the look with an old pair of brown corduroys and her old red boots.

It was actually beginning to smell like winter. The cold air invigorated her as she stepped outside. Since Jenny and Chris lived less than a mile away, she decided to walk. The night air was crisp but temperatures hovered in the low sixties so the outdoor fireplace would feel good. Catching up with Dan as soon as she made it to their friends' driveway, she couldn't help but chuckle at the sweater he was sporting.

Covered in reindeer. Literally covered. And the brightest godawful color of green. How fun it was to share even a simple moment like this with him again. She marveled at how handsome she still found him. He was a good foot taller than her five feet, and she could still get lost in his soft blue eyes and quick smile. When they were younger and she had dreamt about their future kids, she always pictured them with his eyes. Snapping back to the present, she joined him in greeting their friends in the backyard where they enjoyed eggnog and snacks around the fireplace.

When they found a quiet moment, he approached her with his taste testing/puzzle evenings idea. Surprisingly unguarded, she said she'd love to spend several evenings doing just that. She let the thought creep in that maybe they did still have a second chance after all. "Okay," he suggested, "Let's start tomorrow night. We can catch up for a couple evenings before Winter Stroll. Take a bit of a breather and have some quieter nights together. Just the two of us." Yup. Maybe they did have a chance.

Meanwhile, Maggie had invited Jack to dinner that evening. He was easy to talk to and easy on the eyes. She wanted to get to know him better. All she knew about him was that he had been in private practice in Chicago until he moved here. She hoped he would share more about himself with her.

Dinner was already prepared so she could relax with him when he arrived. She had decided to keep it simple and had made a spicy vegetable soup, dinner rolls, salad, and for dessert she bought cheesecake from the bakery. Balance. She hoped he wasn't too strict with his diet. She smiled at the possibility. More for her if he was. A bottle of Sauvignon Blanc was chilled and opened on the counter. Her ex had never enjoyed wine with her. Beer only for him. She wouldn't necessarily mind if Jack didn't want to drink it, but she had always had this silly fantasy that she could open a bottle and share it with someone. Someday.

Maggie was as dressed up as she had been in a while in comfortable yet chic black and white loose flowing slacks and kaftan. She was barefoot as usual, but she had painted her toenails cherry red for the occasion and had worn red lipstick as well, a nod to the special way she felt about tonight.

Jack arrived with a gift of flowers Tammy had helped him select at her flower shop. White roses and baby's breath in a tall mason jar, wrapped in twine, exactly what she knew Maggie would choose herself. Dressed in a button down light blue shirt under a navy pullover sweater and olive khakis, Jack looked handsome and comfortable as he handed her the bouquet. She was thankful for the flowers but more grateful to smile back at the ruggedly handsome man a few inches taller than her with twinkling blue eyes and an easy smile. Something deep inside her had been telling her for years that a man with a smile that crinkled his eyes and so real that it lit his face, somehow that was what she wanted to find in a companion.

"Come in out of the cold; the bouquet is lovely," she invited him in and encouraged him to kick off his shoes and relax on the couch. "Or you can leave your shoes on. My rules are not as strict as they are at the studio. I never want a student to faceplant on the floor where someone has tracked in the outside."

"Thanks, Maggie, you look lovelier than the bouquet and your home is so inviting. I'm happy to kick off my shoes. Not a fancy guy."

"Don't make me blush. I was just about to pour myself a glass of white wine. Does that sound good to you or would you prefer a beer?"

"A glass of white sounds just right. May I pour it for us?"

"Sure, come into the kitchen with me." She led the way through the dining room. Her home was one of the oldest craftsmen in town, close to a hundred years old and she had lived there since Kate was three. Over the years she had made it her own, decorating one room at a time. She was a big fan of antique shops and resale, the kitschier the better. Maggie never knew what she was looking for until she lay eyes on it. Then she would buy it, knowing if she were drawn to it, the piece would work somewhere in her home. She was actually a little disappointed that the place was full now. She felt the itch to decorate again.

The kitchen was her favorite room in the house. Not overly large, but appointed just as she liked. She wouldn't call herself a minimalist in her design taste, but she did like things simple, with a few unique Bohemian touches here and there. The original hardwood floor continued into the kitchen; small rag rugs created warmth underfoot. Walnut stained butcher block kitchen counters were offset by the white subway tile that reached to the ceiling. One wall had been converted to open shelving where plants were interspersed with large glass jars of dried beans, spices, coffee, rice, quinoa, sugar, flour, and more. The other cupboards were painted a pale gray blue. The sink was original farmhouse and the effect was warm, inviting, cozy and as unpretentious as the owner. Maggie perched on a barstool at the island as Jack poured their wine.

"Cheers," he toasted as he handed her a glass and they sat down at the island.

Maggie took a sip and thought about how at home she felt with this man. Whoa, she told herself. Slow down. You hardly know him. Don't make the same mistake twice.

They chatted easily in the comfortable room, surrounded by the enticing food smells of simmering soup and freshly baked rolls. She was in no rush to eat but more than eager to learn more about him.

"Tell me about yourself. What brings you from Chicago to our little town?"

"I wanted a different life," he shared. He went on to openly let her in on the events that had unfolded, eventually bringing him to Beacon.

His eyes darkened, saddened, "My wife passed away five years ago, after a short fight with lung cancer. She never smoked and lived a healthy lifestyle. My colleagues and I did everything we could to save her. It was devastating. I felt like a failure, inept, she was the love of my life and I could do nothing to save her."

Maggie took his hand in hers, "I'm so sorry." She had no other words, knowing her silence would express compassion better than empty platitudes.

"It took two years before I was anything more than a robot, going through the motions, and trying not to feel," he admitted. "And the past three years I have been slowly reaching for the light, climbing out of the dark hole I was in. Whew, I didn't mean to get so heavy. Not very good banter for sharing a glass of wine with a beautiful woman. Sorry."

She looked deeply into his eyes and her warm smile told him she was open to anything he wanted to share with her.

"Let's take our salads to the dining room," she offered.

"Or we can just stay here in your inviting kitchen," he suggested. "I feel so at home here."

She served the salads on the island. Then the soup and rolls, then the dessert with decaf coffee.

The conversation flowed easily and was lighter.

"I've lived in Beacon my whole life. Where did you grow up, near Chicago?"

"Actually," he told her, "I grew up in a small town in Iowa not far from the Mississippi River.

Not as small as Beacon, but a town where Midwest values were instilled in me from an early age.

Would you believe it? I was a wrestler in high school and college."

"I don't know much about wrestling," she said. "Basketball is the big deal here."

"Oh, I wanted to play basketball too, but I'm height challenged as you can see," he replied.

She thought to herself that his height was just fine with her.

Maggie couldn't remember a night she had spent with such a charming, interesting man in at least a decade. He invited her to join him for the Holiday Stroll. She had to work it from the yoga studio so she couldn't, but he offered to help her. And they agreed they would spend some time together afterward.

Back at Dan's childhood home, the puzzle he had chosen reminded Kate of the town village, except colder, somewhere with a true winter. That was all the snow Kate needed to see. It didn't have to be in person. Well maybe on Christmas Eve it would be lovely, but the rare Carolina snow was more likely to fall on a random morning in February or March. Last year it had snowed midweek in April. Of course, it melted as fast as it fell.

While Dan put the finishing touches on his famous hot turkey sandwiches, she sorted through the box for all the edge pieces. Why did it seem like no matter how carefully she sorted through the pieces, it always took two or three runs through the box? Maybe she'd be lucky this time.

"Dinner's ready," Dan called from the kitchen. "Get it while it's hot!"

"It's delicious, easily my favorite comfort food," Kate managed the compliment between bites. "Did I ever tell you about mom craving it while she was pregnant with me? Morning noon or night for the first three months it was all she could stomach. Dad used to take her out to the diner so she could eat something." He hadn't remembered the story.

"No wonder you love it so much! And for dessert, hope you're still hungry. Texas sheet cake with homemade vanilla ice cream."

"Wow Dan, I'm going to gain weight eating like this. Guess I'll just run more often. You'd like that, huh Freddie?" She ruffled her dog's fur.

"Kate, you look perfect the way you are. And I can't imagine a few more pounds could change that fact."

"Keep the compliments coming and I won't ask you to dig around for the missing puzzle edges if I didn't find them all. Let me do the dishes since you cooked and you relax by the fire to work on it."

"Deal."

The fire was crackling and the puzzle border pieces were spread out on the coffee table close to the fireplace. Dan was digging through the box searching for stray edge pieces.

After she finished up in the kitchen, Kate tried to concentrate on the puzzle, but her full belly and the warmth from the fire made her drowsy. In spite of herself, she was relaxing, enjoying the evening. She reclined on the couch just to rest her eyes.

RECIPE

Texas sheet cake recipe (easiest, best chocolate cake you will ever eat)

- Lightly grease a 10 by 15 jelly roll pan

- Preheat oven to 350 degrees

Cake:

- 2 c white flour

- 2 c white sugar

- 1 t. baking soda

- ¼ t salt

- 1 t. cinnamon

- ¾ c water

- 2 sticks of butter

- ¼ c dark cocoa powder

- ½ c buttermilk

- t. vanilla

- 2 large eggs beaten

Directions

- Melt butter, cocoa, water. Bring to rapid boil and pour over sugar and flour mixture. Mix well and add baking soda, cinnamon, salt, buttermilk, eggs and vanilla.

- Pour into the pan and bake for around 20 minutes.

Frosting:

- Stick of butter

- 1/3 c buttermilk

- ¼ c dark cocoa powder

- 3 ¼ c powdered sugar

- ½ cup chopped pecans (optional)

- 2 t vanilla

Directions

- While the cake is baking, bring butter, milk and cocoa to a boil, remove from heat and add powdered sugar and stir until smooth. Add vanilla and nuts if you like them.

- Pour over the cake right when it comes out of the oven.

Chapter 12

The next thing Kate knew she was opening her eyes. She discovered herself covered in a couple of soft quilts. The sun was starting to peek through the window blinds. Dan had placed the blankets on her last night and slipped a pillow from his bed under her head, left her asleep on the couch. Freddie had snuck up and slept at her feet. Maybe she ought to feel embarrassed or uneasy or at the least self-conscious, but all she felt was rested. She didn't even look in a mirror, just wiped the sleep from her eyes.

The enticing smell of coffee had prodded her awake. Dan brought two mugs full to the couch.

"Morning sleepyhead." He handed her a coffee and as their hands brushed, she felt a few of the old familiar sparks. She tried to ignore the feeling. And he was thinking to himself how unpretentious she seemed. He found it refreshing.

Morning. She thought, I could get used to this. "What time is it?" She managed as she stretched her arms over her head and tried unsuccessfully to stifle a yawn.

"Only six thirty, sit back and relax. I took Freddie out for a quick run. You don't teach until nine, right? Plenty of time to ease into the morning."

She settled back on the couch cushions not even caring about her bed head and yesterday's clothes. Yes. She could definitely get used to this. And maybe, just maybe, he had changed.

He felt like the boy she knew so many years ago. She wished she could be sure.

"What's the big smile?" he asked.

"Oh. I guess I'm just a morning person," she teased.

"Well, enjoy that coffee and stay as late as you'd like. Make yourself at home. I'm off to the café. Got some fixtures arriving this morning." He kissed the top of her head. "See you at dinner time."

"See you then."

After he left, Kate poured another cup of coffee and rummaged through the kitchen junk drawer until she found note paper and a pen. Returning to her nest on the couch, she set her coffee on the side table and started writing the story that she needed to examine. She tried to stick to the facts and keep her emotion out of it so she wouldn't have to cross so much off this time.

He went off to Duke. She thought he would come back after. He didn't.

Ten years later he showed up, is changing careers, doing what she thought he would years ago, opening the café.

They had both changed in the meantime.

He took care of her when she sprained her ankle.

He decorated the Christmas tree with her mom.

He walked Freddie when she couldn't.

He came to yoga!

He cooked her favorite foods for her.

He offered to co-host the village party.

And then he was incredible last night and this morning.

She felt at home with him.

She looked back over what she had written. There was nothing to cross out but plenty to smile about. Still part of her felt wary. She couldn't help but doubt her feelings and thoughts about what they have. After all, she thought they'd had it before. She's independent now. This is nice, but for how long? She doesn't want to start all over again if he does leave. She would love to believe in their future together, but she can't quite yet. Was she falling in love with him again? Had she ever fallen out? Could she trust the relationship to last this time? In a little over a week? More questions than answers.

Her cell phone alerted her to a text. Jenny. "Usual place at 7:30?"

"Sure," she replied back.

She had plenty to talk about with her best friend.

After walking home and taking a quick shower, Kate arrived at the coffee shop dressed in her yoga clothes so she'd be prepared to teach at nine. Her wardrobe was pretty standard, almost like a uniform, but a comfortable one. She owned several pairs of solid leggings, mostly black, and she usually wore gray, white, or black yoga tops. She could throw on any color of long sweater or tunic and be ready to go pretty much anywhere. She might even dress that way if she didn't teach yoga. So comfortable, she knew several women who did. Today she got fancy and added a gray knit scarf to her white sleeveless tank and black fitted pants, topped with a gray and white long oversized sweater.

Jenny greeted her. "Wow, what's with the big smile? You're practically outshining the holiday lights!"

She was the second one to ask her that question this morning. Had she not been smiley before?

Standing in line for their coffees they chatted about Adam and Tyler's anticipation for Santa and the work Chris was doing to scrounge up cafe tables. "I think he likes the hunt for all the different tables that he can cobble together and form a seating arrangement to help Dan find a cozy look for the café," Jenny said. "He is enjoying the break from routine and you know he has always been high energy."

Once they sat down with their coffees and breakfast pastries, Jenny crossed her long legs and settled in. She stared into her friend's happy hazel eyes. "Spill!"

Kate took a deep breath. She stretched her arms out, then hugged herself protectively before admitting, "I think I'm still a little bit in love with him. But it scares me. My heart is falling for him, but my head says slow down."

"Is he giving you signals that he might be feeling the same way you do?"

Kate found herself smiling even though she was trying not to.

She wasn't going there. Not out loud anyway.

Holiday Stroll was tomorrow night. The day flew by as Kate and Dan both had details to finalize for the event. He was eager to serve the hot chocolate flights. Even though there wouldn't be tables in the café yet, he could open his doors and sample hot chocolate. The flights would include raspberry, pumpkin spice, peanut butter, almond, and salted caramel. He'd offer it to Kate tonight and serve a cheese and fruit plate as they worked on the puzzle by the fireplace. Just the thought of another evening with her alone at home inspired him to keep working hard. He wanted to talk to her about his need to find a new place to live. His dad would be back from London in a week, and there was no way Dan could live in the same house with him. He wondered again how he could have been so overly influenced by his father when underneath it all they were so different.

The parent child relationship is complicated. Why do grown adults continue to live their lives to please parents that haven't necessarily even been good role models? Darn it. Dan wasn't the one to ask, that's for sure. His thoughts returned to the hot chocolate flavors and creating the recipes. Plenty to plan and ingredients to buy if he was going to serve the first flight to Kate tonight. He needed to get the ingredients for the fruit and cheese plate. Since it was winter, he decided on apples, dates, grapes, and pears. For the cheese he would heat up brie in a flakey crust, top it with warmed fig jam and serve it with sesame crackers on the side. He'd sprinkle in some almonds and cashews too.

Later that evening, once they'd cleared another delicious dinner and sat down by the fireplace for a hot chocolate flight, he brought up his idea for a place he could live. He'd been chomping at the bit to get her input. He was also more than a little concerned she might think he was crazy. He hadn't yet shared his idea with anyone. He took a deep breath.

"Kate, you know I need to find a new place of my own. I just can't stay in this house for ten minutes once my dad returns from London."

"I get that, Dan. Your dad can be um, how can I put it, challenging."

"To say the least, Kate! My idea is... drumroll please. I want to buy the old Wilson house on the corner."

"Wow, Dan, I'm surprised. You want to tackle that old place at the same time as you are getting the café up and running? Your plate might be overfull, and she couldn't help but change the subject... this salted caramel hot chocolate. Amazing."

"Thanks. I hope you like them all, but back to the Wilson house. Kate, I get it, but I've always done better when I keep busy. And I've wanted to renovate an old place for a long time. How many times did we walk by that house as high school kids and you would talk nonstop about wondering what it would be like to live in it? I have to tell you that I thought you were nuts back then. But, now... I wouldn't do much at first. Just make a corner of it livable for myself. Think about it, only a block from the village. The ideal spot for a B&B."

"Oh my gosh, a B&B! Even more work. Long term commitment work. You must be planning to make this town your own again." She couldn't keep herself from lovingly jabbing his side.

"Hey, what can I say," he answered. "Those HGTV shows are giving me a few ideas of my own. And yes, I'm here for good." Their eyes met and she found herself falling even more deeply in spite of herself.

"Well, I think it's exciting. But if you're sure that you want to purchase it, can you hop on it right away? The place is bound to have multiple offers. It's the best location in town for a B&B. And the charm of the place. Imagine what it was like over a hundred and sixty years ago. There must be old pictures. It had to be grand and it could be again. My opinion is a resounding YES. Why not? You're right. I have loved it forever. With the brewery opening across the street and everything else in the village, we have visitors driving down from Charlotte every weekend seeking the quaint charm of Beacon. Some of them are bound to want to make a weekend if it, maybe even take a yoga class while they're here, check out the shops, enjoy the café and Riggio's once they are up and running again. They can't do everything Beacon has to offer in just one day." Her wheels were turning.

"I'd help if you wanted me to and Aunt Ali would be an amazing resource. She's been itching to renovate more than their house. Mom is a good decorator too and I think she's been a little eager to decorate again now that her place is as full as she wants it. You would have plenty of help. Maybe you should call Jenny right now," she encouraged him.

"Why not? You only live once. I'm going for it now that you're on board."

He reached Jenny by phone and told her of his interest in the old Wilson place.

She responded with the info he had expected.

"Jenny, yeah. I know the asking price won't be the going price. What if we go fifteen grand over asking? I'm thinking some of the other offers may go over by five or ten. And how about we write a letter stating my intentions? Maybe it'll help that I'm a hometown boy who wants to turn it into a B&B."

"Can't hurt, Dan. If you're sure, I'll write up the offer."

"I'm sure, Jenny. Talk soon." He could hardly believe how sure he was.

"Ok, Kate. Now we wait. Let's give this puzzle a go. I'm energized. And not just from the cocoa either."

"Which, Dan, is excellent. I don't even know which one is my favorite. Better make tons for tomorrow."

Their attention turned to the holiday scene they were attempting to put together on the coffee table.

Chapter 13

Winter Stroll mostly kept Kate and Dan tending to their own businesses. Kate did manage to take a break and check out how things were going at the café. Dan and a couple of Riggio's employees were making hot chocolate flights and serving them as fast as they could. Now that the night air had turned cold, customers were lining up outside the doors to wait for their turn. Word was spreading fast about the new café to open soon and about the delicious hot cocoa flights.

Kate wanted to help out so she ran back into the studio to make sure her mom could spare her for a few minutes. "Dan is really busy. People are lined up down the street. Can you let me go so I can help out?"

"Sure, Katie girl, things are well under control. And Jack is here." She smiled at him. "Much more interest in hot chocolate on a night like this anyway. Go on over and help out."

Not having to be told twice, Kate rushed back into the café, grabbed an apron and pitched in. All the flavors appeared to be a hit and Dan was definitely going to want these on the menu for the winter season. She was in charge of adding the whipped cream to each one, and she felt like Freddie should be at her side. He was always there at the ready every single time for his whipped topping treat. She drank hot cocoa practically every night in the winter, and as soon as she grabbed the can from her fridge, he would hear the nozzle spray and appear in a flash to get a taste of his own, usually licking it off his nose. Who was she kidding, she would be licking it off her own nose too.

Jenny popped in to have a flight of cocoa. She also saw the need for help, and took a break from the general store to pitch in. She had some tentative news about the Wilson house and wanted to give Dan an update. Peeking around the wall to the kitchen, she waited until she had his attention. "Things are looking promising on the purchase of the Wilson house; we should know by late tomorrow afternoon." Deep into the production of cocoa, he returned the news with a nod and a broad smile.

The Victorian farmhouse was one of the oldest in town, built in 1849 for George Wilson, a prominent Beacon citizen and banker in those days. Four generations were raised in that beautiful home, but in the last fifteen years or so, it had fallen into disrepair with none of the family members in this generation wanting to stay in Beacon. Standing on the corner of Main and Providence, the location was ideal for a B&B, just a block from the village. He could practically throw a stone and hit the café from there. And the grounds were vast, filled with shade trees where guests would be able to relax and sip lemonade or sweet tea on a hot summer day. He could visualize shade gardens and meandering paths providing respite after a busy day spent visiting the village. A fire pit, maybe a gazebo.

He could hardly wait until late tomorrow afternoon. The evening had been a success and that was something to celebrate.

As soon as he closed for the night and the others left, Dan and Kate propped themselves up on the counter to rest. Dan was antsy though, couldn't relax. He was too amped up about the house. It really was in bad shape. He had to be realistic. Before any guests would be enjoying the grounds, that house had to be totally renovated, inside and out. He recalled George Bailey's house in 'It's a Wonderful Life.' In its present condition, the Wilson house looked like the "before" of the Bailey home. Still, he wanted to walk over and look at it. Right now.

"Kate, let's close this place and go take a look at the Wilson house."

"Sure, I guess," she said with some hesitation in her voice, "but we walk by it every day on the way to our homes. Why do you want to stare at it on a cold night?"

"Because I'm seeing it restored in my mind. And I just have to go see it now. Oh, man, I'm afraid I might be getting really spontaneous."

"And spontaneity looks good on you. Whatever happened to slow and steady wins the race? Oh, never mind," she liked seeing that in him. Kate grabbed her coat and stocking hat. "Let's go!"

As they stood bundled in the cold night air on the sidewalk in front of the house that Dan hoped to own tomorrow, he was flooded with thoughts of what it could be. Kate was regarding it in her own mind too. She tried to be the realist but remembered how she had felt when she and her mom opened Beacon Yoga.

"I've always loved this black iron fence," she offered aloud, "can't believe the detail."

"Me too. And I like that it's only picket fence high," Dan agreed. "But I was looking at the peeling paint. And the shutters hanging askew on most of the windows. And… Oh well, let me walk you home. We won't know if it's mine until tomorrow night anyway." He attempted to stifle his excitement with practicality.

Arriving at Kate's, they both realized they were too keyed up to say goodnight.

"You ready to call it a night?" he asked, hoping she wanted to spend more time with him.

"Not really." They kept walking, enjoying homes decorated with Christmas lights, now and then commenting on one that stood out above the rest. The village was blanketed in white lights. Every roof, window, doorframe outlined, every tree branch, every tree trunk. The effect was magical and they were drawn in that direction.

The horse drawn carriage that had been offering rides during Winter Stroll was just getting ready to retire for the night. Impulsively, Dan inquired if he could hire them for one more ride. He spoke quietly to the driver for a moment, then assisted Kate up into the carriage. Covering the two of them in a heavy blanket, he settled into the seat and nestled in beside her.

The usual ride took passengers throughout the village, but Dan had paid extra for the driver to take a longer route. He found Kate's hand and held it in his as they rode through the village and out onto the streets of Beacon. She squeezed his hand a little tighter through her gloved hand.

"Do you remember the rides we used to take through the village back in high school?" Kate questioned. Those were some of her best memories. "I haven't done this since then, have you?"

He shook his head. "Nope."

"Dan," Kate asked quietly as the horses led them by the Methodist church, "Have I ever told you my very favorite childhood Christmas memory?"

"I'm not sure, tell me."

"Well, my mom and I always went to Christmas Eve midnight services at this church."

"With your mom and dad, you mean?"

"No, my dad always stayed home."

"I'm sorry," he gently offered.

"No, it's okay. But the thing that made it the best was, just as Christmas Eve was becoming Christmas, everyone in the darkened sanctuary would sing my favorite carol, 'Silent Night,' and the church slowly filled with candlelight, symbolizing the light Jesus brought to the world. I can't describe the beauty, the feelings it evoked."

"And you don't usually go now?"

"We have been so caught up in the village Christmas party. I think without meaning to, we have just let the tradition go." They continued to enjoy the clear starry night before the horses deposited them back at Kate's bungalow. Thanking her for a lovely evening. he kissed the top of her head, ran his fingers through Freddie's fur, kissed the top of his head, and went home for the night. She couldn't help but wonder when he might make his way from the top of her head to her lips.

Maggie and Jack had closed the yoga studio and had taken their own saunter out on the village paths under the lights. Nice to be out after the stroll alone, just the two of them, he asked her to tell him about herself.

"Well, the yoga studio came about nine years ago after my ex-husband decided he needed a new life and a younger model. Rough time as it was, and Kate only eighteen when we started the new chapter, I love my life now." She smiled up at his baby blues. "I know you get it; when did you start practicing yoga?"

Sadness darkened his eyes as he told her it was after his wife's passing. His daughters, both grown now, had been doing yoga for years and thought it would help his healing. He had been astonished at what it brought up for him. His teachers told him that who you are on your mat is a reflection of who you are off your mat. He learned so much about himself. He realized he was a control freak, wanting to perfect each yoga pose, holding his breath to achieve more, the opposite of what yoga was teaching him: to let go, to watch each deep inhale and exhale.

"You've come a long way then. I can tell you focus on breath and that you move in and out of the poses with ease, that it isn't about how it looks for you. Tell me more about your daughters."

"They're the reason I am here. Both of them live in Charlotte, only twenty minutes away in Ballantine. Susan is married, no kids yet. Jen is married and has the cutest, smartest little two-year-old boy that you have ever seen. I can't get enough of him. Plus, I wanted the small-town atmosphere after Chicago and once I visited all the little rural communities, I was sold on Beacon. Your studio was a big reason, and then getting the chance to work at the clinic. Done deal. My place is just around the corner in the village apartments. After Chicago, I love that I can practically walk everywhere here. Say, would you like to come over for a nightcap?"

"What the heck, why not?" she instantly replied.

Saturday found Dan and Kate busy with separate endeavors before they caught up with each other for the late afternoon yoga class they had planned to take together. Usually, the class was full of couples practicing before they went out for the evening, or more likely, home to their kids.

Jenny and Chris were there today, along with Andy and Amy. Dan gave Jenny a questioning, and at the same time, hopeful look.

"Nope. Sorry haven't heard yet," she answered his unasked query.

Maggie guided the class through a powerful flow and before they knew it, class was over.

As they assembled in the lobby to get ready to head out, Dan saw Jenny pick up her cell phone to retrieve voice mails.

He tried to ignore her while he waited with anticipation, well, actually worry and anxiety were more like it.

Jenny rushed over and the grin spreading across her face said it all.

"It's mine?"

"All yours. Offer was accepted."

He pivoted to Kate and embraced her, elated at the turn his life was taking.

"Jenny, do you know when I take possession?"

She checked her message again. "First of the year, technically, but I told them you'd want in as early as possible so you'd be able to move in while you work on it. Since no one has lived there for years, they agreed. So, you can go in and assess the place as early as tomorrow."

"Perfect. Thanks for all your hard work. I owe you one."

"We're friends, Dan. It always evens out in the end. No worries."

Jack was tying his tennis shoes nearby.

"Dan, did I overhear that you are planning to turn that old house on the corner into a B&B?'

"Call me crazy, Jack, but yes, I am."

"Doesn't sound crazy to me. The minute I saw that place I thought the same thing. If I were your age, I might have gone for it myself. What a perfect location. What kind of shape is it in?"

"Not the best, but wiring and plumbing, even the roof, are in surprisingly good condition."

"I'd love to take a look at it sometime if that's okay; I'm intrigued by the place."

"Sure, how is Monday for you, around lunchtime?"

"I'll be there."

RECIPE

Hot chocolate basic recipe: makes one serving

- Pour 1 mug almost full of the milk of your choice

- Add one heaping tablespoon of the best dark chocolate powder you can find

- Add two heaping tablespoons of cane sugar.

- Stir.

- Microwave one minute, Stir. Microwave one more minute.

- Add ½ t. vanilla and top with your favorite whipped cream.

- Raspberry version:

- Stir in 2 tsp of raspberry jam when you add the vanilla.

Pumpkin spice version:

- Add ½ t. or more to taste when you add the vanilla.

Peanut butter version

- Add 1 to 2 tsp. peanut butter when you add the vanilla. Sprinkle a small handful of finely chopped peanuts on top of the whipped cream.

Almond version:

- Add ½ t. almond extract when you add the vanilla.

Salted caramel version:

- Drizzle melted caramel sauce on top, you choose the amount. Sprinkle with sea salt.

Chapter 14

Dan picked up Kate at the crack of dawn Sunday morning to go over to the Wilson, no, make that the Ivy house. He wanted her with him when he went inside for the first time as owner.

She met him at the door already bundled in her coat and winter boots, as eager as he was to get inside the old place. On the walk over she asked him, "How are you doing with it all? Could you get any sleep last night?"

He replied without hesitation that he couldn't be more ready for this new chapter. "My life before coming back here was never really me. I don't know why I was living that way. Maybe still the little boy in me trying to impress my dad. It might sound crazy to hear me say this, but I feel free for the first time in my life."

"You're going into debt and starting two businesses so to the casual observer that would sound crazy, but not to me. You feel like the old Dan."

Arriving at the gate to Dan's home and the future B&B, they practically ran to the front entrance.

As the door literally creaked open, the two of them stepped inside and stared at the magnificent staircase. Even covered in layers of dust and strung with Halloween-like cobwebs they could see the beauty underneath. Walking to the right through the front room, massive light-filled dining room, and utilitarian but perfectly doable kitchen, they made their way to the space Dan needed to ready so he could move in. Just past the back staircase was a small bathroom outfitted with a clawfoot tub, sink and toilet. A wonderful sunroom that would serve as a temporary living room/office for Dan was adjacent to the bath. The back door opened to an old side porch, and beyond the porch lay the expansive yard, overgrown, but they could see the promise of beautiful summer gardens. Through the kitchen behind the sunroom was a bedroom and adequate closet.

"All this is going to take is some elbow grease. We can have these rooms ready for you in no time at all," Kate suggested characteristically optimistic.

The rest of the house was perfectly laid out for a B&B, with a spacious living room to the left of the front entry and six bedrooms upstairs with two bathrooms for guests to share. The old home had good bones and just needed some refreshing. Kate was raring to get started.

"Let's grab a coffee and chocolate croissants at the coffee shop, then head to my house for cleaning supplies. I'm ready to get the place cleaned up so you can move in."

He gave her an incredulous look. "You want to spend Sunday cleaning this house?"

"Of course. What are friends for?"

Giving her a big hug, his unspoken thoughts were about far more than friendship.

"I'm ready if you are. Lead on."

By nine a.m. they were attacking the rooms he would call home with a vengeance. Dan tackled the bathroom while Kate started on his bedroom. Relieved that the home was partially furnished, she found the old iron bed charming and the chest of drawers would suffice for the time being, but the old drapes would have to go. She dragged down the dust filled, heavy black velvet drapery and hauled them out the back door.

Returning to the bedroom she was greeted with the welcome sight of light spilling in through the old blinds. Throwing out the musty bedding and mattress cover, she was left with a bare bones room that she could clean top to bottom. A couple hours later as she swept the wood floors, she was satisfied that Dan could soon sleep in this bedroom. Kate and Maggie could easily outfit the bed with comfy bedding and pillows. Dan had the bathroom clean as well and was starting to wash the sunroom windows.

"This isn't taking as long as I thought it would. You can probably sleep here tonight. I'm going to see if any of the kitchen appliances still work."

"Kate, you're a speed demon, but that's enough work for today. I think we ought to enjoy the rest of this afternoon."

"I'd like nothing better than to enjoy the day by working on the café, Dan. We have a party there on Christmas Eve."

"You're right. And you're the best." He only hesitated momentarily. "What did you have in mind?"

Arriving at his café, he found out what she had in mind.

"How did you get in here?" He turned to the Spring's and several other old friends.

"I'm your realtor, Dan. It was not that hard, and unless you want to press charges…" Jenny laughed.

He stood in the doorway mouth agape at all the tables and chairs his friends had scattered around the room.

"I don't even have words," he managed.

The saying that old friends are the best friends was certainly true in this case.

Chris had found more than tables and chairs. The place was transformed into a café.

Dan's gaze took in pictures of special Beacon landmarks, the high school gymnasium, the town square, the old Wilson property, and he managed to speak. "I could never have done any of this myself. I'm almost speechless. Everyone, please take a seat. Lunch is on the house." He disappeared into the kitchen to thank them the best way he knew how.

They soon made themselves at home. Heading over to the shelf that held books and games that Chris had found, his friends started playing Monopoly at one table, Scrabble at another.

Kate took their beverage requests and sat down to join the threesome at the Scrabble table.

What an amazing day it was turning out to be.

Before they knew it, Dan was at the counter with grilled cheese and tomato soup for the crowd. They eagerly grabbed their lunches and sat down to feast on a well-deserved thank you meal. And the afternoon flew by with all present enjoying old fashioned board games. Once everyone left for home and Dan had an open opportunity, he was ready to tell Kate about his old relationship with Belinda. He didn't want anything in his past to come between him and Kate and their future together. Before the words could spill, he looked up to see Maggie and Ali laden with more food deliveries. The talk would have to wait. Plenty of time. But this food delivery had to be shelved.

"Whew, what a full day!" I can't believe everything we accomplished, but I'm beat," Kate admitted. Dan agreed. Now that the two of them were alone, he suggested they head back to his dad's house to relax by the fire. And there in the living room, not a welcome sight at all, was Dan's father. He was the very last person Dan wanted to see at the end of a long day, and from the look on Harold's face, he must have felt the same way seeing the two of them.

"Dad, I didn't expect you home already."

"Obviously, it seems by the puzzle and what I've seen in the kitchen, the two of you have made yourselves at home." He didn't sound pleased.

"Don't worry Dad. We're out." The day had been too full to expend any remaining energy on him.

They shut the door and stood on the front steps, exhausted.

"What do we do now?" Dan asked Kate.

She took his hand in hers. "Walk me home. We'll figure it out."

"Just for tonight," Kate assured him as she dressed the couch as a bed. "Tomorrow we will outfit your new bedroom at the Ivy Place." He thanked her and lay down, too tired to refuse.

"See you in the morning, then," he smiled. And stretching out on the couch, he fell into the most restful night's sleep he'd had in a long, long time.

Chapter 15

"Good morning. Can't guarantee my coffee is as good as yours, but here you go," she handed him a mug of coffee.

"I could get used to this, thanks, how did you sleep?" he asked taking a sip of the java.

She had slept well. But today was a busy one at the yoga studio. She had two classes to teach.

"Got to head to the studio, make yourself at home. Catch up with you soon. Mom said something about helping you get your bedroom set up today if you have the time.

She'll give you a call this morning." She and Freddie were out the door.

"Oh, Mrs. Nola, your car is full, you're being too good to me," he exclaimed as the two of them stood looking at everything she had brought over for his bedroom.

"Ok, Dan. It's time to call me Maggie, please."

"Got it. You've got yourself a deal, Maggie. Let's pull up to the back door so it will be easy to unload."

She pulled the car up to the back entrance and before they unpacked it, he gave her a tour of the home. Just as they were finishing up, Jack came striding through the gate. He and Dan unloaded Maggie's car.

"Pleasant surprise seeing you, and perfect timing. Thanks for helping," she thanked Jack and the two men started touring the house as Maggie began working her magic creating a comfortable and welcoming bed for him. She had Dan bring in a couple of end tables from the living room and added the lamps she brought to provide bedside light.

"Dan, you made a wise decision purchasing this place. The potential is phenomenal. I'd like to invest if you decide you want a partner," Jack offered.

"Really? That sure gives me something to think about. Say, I'm making chili tonight. Can you join us?"

"I would never turn that down. I've got patients to see at one thirty so I need to get back to the clinic. See you tonight then." He said his goodbyes to Dan and Maggie.

"I think I may have a good oval woven rug in the attic, Dan. It would provide some warmth for your feet. I'll bring it next time if you'd like."

"I'd like. But let me get it out of your attic. No more ankle injuries for the Nola women," he insisted. "Thanks again. And I'm planning to make a big pot of chili for dinner tonight. The stove and fridge are old, but they work. Please come back for dinner. It's the least I can do."

"I'd love to." She readily accepted. "See you later, then."

Dan made a spicy chili, cornbread, and apple crisp for dinner. Kate and Maggie came over after Kate's classes wrapped up. They were pleasantly surprised to see how clean Dan had managed to get the kitchen that afternoon. Not up to date, but serviceable and spotless, he could definitely move in and make it work until he could convert it into a kitchen more suitable for the B&B. After dinner he'd grab his belongings from his dad's and be ready to officially stay the night.

Maggie had brought towels and a bathmat for the bathroom so he'd have everything he needed.

"Hey, man, come on in." Dan welcomed Jack into the kitchen and noticed that Jack and Maggie were obviously delighted to be sharing dinner again. Kate was probably even more pleased. Now she could see how the two were interacting firsthand. Her mom had been unbelievably secretive about Jack so far.

Dinner was delicious and his guests suggested he make the chili one of the daily winter soup specials. He agreed and said he would add it to the menu. Conversation flowed smoothly among the four of them. It felt like old times, and Jack fit right in. As they said their goodbyes for the evening, Dan realized how tired he was and headed straight to his new bedroom. Goldilocks could not have been happier than he was now when she crawled into bed at the bears' house.

Saying goodbye to Jack, Kate found some welcome alone time with her mom.

"Walk in the village with me and Freddie?" She wanted to hear what her mom had to say about the handsome new doc.

"I'd love to," Maggie accepted. "It will give me a chance to digest that delicious meal. You and Dan are really enjoying each other's company. It's easy to see."

"We aren't the only ones."

A grin spread across her mom's pretty face. Even in the night lights, Kate could see her mom was happy. She didn't pry any further. She saw some of her mom's trademark spunkiness inching back into her life. It had been gone for a long time and Kate was thrilled to see her more spontaneous, and happy again. Kate had always been more grounded than her mom and Maggie had brought the impulsive fun. Kind of like when she invited Dan to Thanksgiving, Kate had to admit now. That had been a good idea. Hindsight truly did provide 20/20 vision.

The next morning Dan found his mind wandering around in the past, trying to remember what he'd ever seen in Belinda. His life here was falling so amazingly and almost effortlessly into place. How could he ever have thought he wanted the corporate life or the type of woman Belinda was? She couldn't have been more different from Kate.

Kate was low maintenance; Belinda spent an inordinate amount of time and money on her appearance. Kate valued deep trusted friendships; Belinda was all about networking. You scratch my back and I'll scratch yours. Kate was a homebody. Belinda wanted to go out every night to see and be seen.

Nothing wrong with any of that. She just had different priorities than he did and it took him a long time to realize it. Nothing dramatic or drastic had happened to end their year long relationship. He just gradually had started to miss what he'd had and the hometown lifestyle that reflected the true him. Trying to become who his dad wanted him to be had been a disastrous detour for Dan.

Belinda had been shocked. She hadn't seen the break-up coming, but he had come to know it was definitely over for him. He wished her well, but his feelings for her just weren't there anymore. That was six months ago. He did some soul searching and decided he wanted to come home and open the café. And now the future B&B was his home. He couldn't be happier. And he was falling so hard for Kate. New York City looked great in the rearview mirror.

Well, enough time spent in the past. The café was almost ready to open. He went over and finalized the chalkboard wall menu and realized he would be ready to open for the Christmas Eve party for sure. Why not invite everyone who had made it happen to a dry run this Friday night? He made some calls and sent out an email blast as invites, then sat down to plan the menu. An hour later, the food plan was set. For drinks he'd serve hot apple cider and, why not, champagne. Appetizers would consist of cream cheese topped with hot pepper jelly on crackers, shrimp cocktail with a spicy sauce, and a veggie tray. The soup course would be corn chowder and for the main course, pecan crusted chicken, boiled red potatoes, and a fruity spinach salad with homemade rolls. Dessert: pumpkin pie and whipped cream from scratch.

He hoped everyone could come on three days' notice and asked Tammy at the florist shop to provide small holiday table toppers.

Stopping by his childhood home to pick up a few more belongings, he found his dad in a contentious mood. Buoyed by his nightly bourbon or two, he was on the attack, but Dan was ready this time. As he stood in the doorway, he braced himself for the inevitable onslaught. Still the words did come as a bit of a shock.

"Son, why on earth are you here with your old small-town girlfriend when you could be married by now to a classy city woman like Belinda?"

"Hold on dad, that was a low blow, even for you. Nothing gives you the right..."

"I have every right as your father," he fired back. "I have always known what is good for you and that woman and your career in New York are exactly what you need. Belinda knows what is important in life and she is a smart, capable, driven businesswoman."

"You couldn't be more wrong. I'll come back for my things when you're not here." He backed out of the house, and quietly closed the door.

Returning to his own back porch and entering the old house, he finally exhaled. Let it go, he told himself, or if you can't do that, let it be. He settled into the one easy chair he owned and picked up the novel he was reading. Exhausted, he didn't even call Kate. But he set his alarm to get up and surprise her by showing up for her six am class the next morning. Wednesday was an early day for her. He wanted to take her class, not only to see her, but also because some of the yoga wisdom was starting to sink in. He had left his dad without firing back hard at him as he had been tempted to. And he felt better about himself because of it.

Dan showed up fifteen minutes early for her class, glad he did because the surprised smile on her face made it worth the early wake up. Classes were small at six am, mostly attended by regulars who knew their day would go better after practicing, especially at busy times of the year like now. He guessed that would be the case for himself as well so he rolled out a mat and went through a few easy stretches before Kate came in to teach. Chris came in, quietly closed the door and rolled out his mat next to Dan.

"Hey man, do you usually take this class?" he asked his buddy.

"Every Monday, Wednesday, and Friday. Jenny wouldn't miss a Tuesday or Thursday. We take turns staying home with the kids. It's early but we both feel better and we also get along better if we do."

Dan thought that was impressive and told his friend as much. Maybe he'd establish a morning routine himself as well. He did feel better as he lay in the nap pose called savasana at the end of class, ready to get after the day.

He approached Kate as she was cleaning up the room after class while the other students left to get on with their mornings. "Thanks, Kate. I sure am glad you followed this path. You found your calling with yoga. Do you have time to grab a coffee and croissant at the coffee shop?"

He wanted to finally talk to her about his past relationship with Belinda. He did not want any secrets between them.

"Wish I could, but I'm subbing the eight am today. Rain check?"

"Of course." He kissed the top of her head, felt the sweat from her hair on his lips and didn't even mind it.

"See you soon, "he smiled.

Dang it though. He'd need to bring up his old fiancé another time.

Checking his email while sitting down alone for a vanilla latte and chocolate croissant at the village coffee shop, he was grateful to see so many friends had RSVP'd yes to the Friday night dinner. He went home for a quick bath, wishing the bathroom had a shower. All in good time, he'd add one when he could. Right now, he needed to concentrate on the café. He'd been meaning to order a sign to hang over the front entry.

The Ivy Café. Yup. White clapboard background with the name in forest green Olde English letters. He headed to the signage business in town and placed the order. In his New York life, he had handled most of his business online. He wanted to support locals now. It felt good. They said they could hang it on Friday before the dinner party that night. His friends would be surprised.

When he got to the café around noon, he got a call from Tammy that his centerpieces were ready. By the time he was done prepping for the upcoming dinner, she'd arrived and set them out on the tables. Everything seemed to be falling into place.

Chris stopped in and remarked how great the café was looking.

"Wondered if you have the time to grab a cheeseburger?"

He didn't have to ask twice. The two headed to the best place in the village for greasy burgers, fries and eggnog milkshakes. Once they had wolfed them down, Chris brought up the uncomfortable question of whether he'd been able to talk to Kate about his past.

Jenny had told him she had not heard from Kate about it so he figured the answer was no.

"I tried this morning, but she had to teach the next class. Soon. It's starting to weigh heavy on me."

"Hey, Chris asked, "are you and Kate in for next Friday night?"

Dan confessed that he didn't know what was going on but he'd probably be in. Chris elaborated that they Christmas caroled to retired teachers every year on the Friday night before Christmas. And took turns hosting the group after. Everyone pitched in with treats to share pot luck style afterwards.

"Then sure, I'm in. And I have a huge living room with an awesome wood fireplace for after. I'll host this year if that's okay."

"Great, thanks man."

RECIPE

Spicy vegetarian chili

- large onion chopped

- cloves garlic minced

- T olive oil

- T chili powder

- ¼ t. basil

- ½ t cumin

- 2 medium zucchini chopped

- 2 carrots chopped

- 1 – 28 oz can of tomatoes, chopped and drained

- ! can kidney beans with liquid

- 1 can black beans, drained

- 1 can garbanzo beans, drained

- 1 large can v- 8 juice

- To garnish

- Sour cream

- Cheddar cheese

- Shredded lettuce

- More chopped onion

Directions

- In a large pot, sauté onion and garlic over medium heat about 5 minutes.

- Mix in the spices, zucchini and carrots. Stir about a minute to combine.

- Add the can of v-8, tomatoes, three cans of beans and simmer about a half hour or so on low heat.

- Set out garnishes as topping options.

Chapter 16

Once Jenny had a break from showings and Kate finished teaching, the two volunteered at the giftwrapping fundraiser, along with Amy. It was getting busier every day as more and more people were shopping and then helping out the Riggio's by supporting the fundraiser instead of wrapping their own gifts. As they busied their hands with the task of gift wrapping, the three old friends found time to catch up.

"Adam, Ty, and Scarlet must be really excited about Santa coming, huh?" Kate asked.

"They sure are, and at the same time they get a little too wild this time of year. Have I told you about Chris pretending to have a direct line to Santa? They 'talk' pretty much every day. The boys listen and it helps keep them in line. Pretty funny!"

Amy said Scarlet was also beside herself with anticipation. And she could hardly wait to join the other kids at the village party on Christmas Eve. She had a long list to share with Santa.

Kate wondered silently if and when she might get to be a mom. She loved those three little ones.

"Hey Kate, speaking of the boys, is there any chance you and maybe Dan could help us out with the boys Saturday night? The general store party is that night and our usual sitter works for Chris at the store so we would like her to be able to come to the party."

"Of course. We love the boys. Well, I can't speak for Dan but I definitely will look forward to spending time with them."

"Thanks a bunch, Kate. They'll be excited."

Kate kept wrapping the gifts and the methodical act of wrapping became almost a meditative process for her. Those silent times when her hands were busy seemed to quiet her mind and she started thinking about what she had been like when they were all back in high school together.

If she and Dan had ended up together then, if she had found a school near him without a plan of her own, she doubted she ever would have become who she was today. She was now an independent, strong, confident human being who never would have become who she was without the adversity of losing him back then. She would have been like an extension of who he was, not having the thoughts, opinions, even experiences of her own that made her a worthy individual who could contribute equally to a new relationship. Kind of like one of her favorite song lines, she whispered a prayer that she was thankful for some of the unanswered prayers of the past.

Shanti was turning twenty-nine today, and after she finished up with the gift wrapping, Kate treated her to lunch as she did on her birthday every year. Shanti was naturally thin and in Kate's opinion beautiful in an exotic way. Her thick black hair and milky coffee colored skin gave her a different kind of beauty than the typical southern gal. She was fun and easy going and they always had a great time together. Today would be no exception as they met at Shanti's favorite seafood restaurant for a late lunch. They always lingered for a couple of hours and the first thing on the docket was the one cosmopolitan they each ordered. Shanti took the afternoon off so she wouldn't have to go back to work. It was only one drink, but still…They also ordered calamari and garlic bread to sop up the creamy, buttery sauce, and hopefully some of the alcohol from the martinis.

"Cheers my friend, happy birthday!" They clinked glasses. Carefully. Ever since the year they clinked too hard and the glasses broke and red liquid had spilled all over the tablecloth. Having no shame, they still returned to the same place. They giggled over the memory as they did every year.

"What are your plans for tonight?" Kate asked, her mouth maybe a little too full of calamari, but who cared? It was that good.

"Joe invited me to dinner at his place. He warned me that it might be takeout, said he isn't half the cook that Dan is," she smiled. And took a big bite of the bread.

'How is it going with him?" Kate questioned.

"I like him. I think he likes me. But it isn't love. Not yet. Anyway, we have a good time together and we are fine with taking it slow. Kate, did you know he was married right out of college?"

"No. I didn't. Guess Dan must have thought it would be gossip to share it with me. Why did it end?"

"She fell in love with someone at work, and out of love with Joe. It only lasted two years. That was seven years ago and he hasn't let himself fall in love since then. I don't blame him."

"That sounds really hard. I don't either, but if you two do fall in love, in my opinion, he hits the jackpot."

"Thanks, Kate. Let's order now." And the rest of the lunch was less eventful, but nice.

Kate went home after spending the afternoon with Shanti. She'd been up since five am so she was exhausted even though it was only dinnertime. Her cell rang.

"Dan, what's up?"

"Just had something to tell you about." He let her know he was in on the annual caroling next Friday and that he'd host the after party this year.

"Perfect. I've got something to run by you too. Jenny mentioned that she and Chris need a sitter Saturday night. I said yes and was hoping you might want to help out. I'm sure it would be more fun for the boys too."

He let her know that he was in. He was actually thought it would be nice spending a quiet evening that way.

"Hey, Dan. I'm beyond tired. I think I'll just eat some cereal, go to bed early and curl up with a book tonight. It's been a long day and tomorrow is my annual cousin day."

"I don't think I know about that. It sounds like a big deal," he told her.

"Oh, it is! I'll take pictures. Anyway, it's tomorrow and tomorrow night so I'll see you Friday. I took off Friday, always do after cousin day. Usually, I take it easy, but this year I am going to put my culinary skills to use helping you out, such as those skills are," she laughed. He assured her that he understood. He wasn't used to getting up at five thirty himself.

"Goodnight. Sleep tight. See you Friday then."

She had spent cousin day with the boys the last three years, since Griffin turned seven. The boys loved taking off from school and their parents agreed that it wouldn't hurt them to miss a day and a half. The memories were worth it and it gave Kate a way to give her cousins the gift of an experience rather than more things that might not end up being that special after a couple of weeks anyway. Since the boys were all good students, they didn't miss a beat. They did the same things every year and she was holding her breath a little that Cheydon at sixteen wouldn't tire of it. Luckily, he hadn't yet, and her aunt and uncle appreciated it since they were able to spend that night together Christmas shopping for the boys.

Ever since Kate could remember, her mom had followed the 'three gifts' rule. She bought her something she wanted, something she needed, and something to wear. Kate planned the activities with the boys each year along those same lines. Something they all wanted was a sleepover at a hotel with a swimming pool and a hot tub. She found a hotel in nearby Charlotte that fit the bill. Not only was there a pool, but a game room and room service for breakfast the next morning as well. During the day they chose gifts for other children their age who weren't as fortunate as they were, and she had the boys promise they would think of those kids on Christmas morning. She wanted them to learn that it truly does feel better to give than to receive. They got to pick out something to wear, and they had fun picking out clothes, usually sweatshirts, sometimes tennis shoes, or winter gear. This year she decided they needed to add something new. She kept it a secret.

Kate traded cars with Ali and Justin so there was plenty of room for all of them in her aunt and uncle's van. The boys piled in. Cheydon called shotgun and his younger brothers climbed in back.

"Where do you guys want to go for breakfast?" she asked.

Declan piped up, "Can we go to the same place we went last year?"

"Yeah," Everett jumped in, "the place with the waffle sandwiches and hash browns!" "Griff, Chey, does that sound good to you guys too?" They eagerly agreed. Kate loved the place also. When the boys ordered the waffle/sausage sandwiches she did too, and they were so delicious that she thought she'd better bring Dan here to see what he thought. He might want to add them to his café lineup, maybe put them on the spring menu. She loaded her hash browns with ketchup and greedily gobbled up breakfast, admiring her cousins' good manners as they ate.

"Now, let's hit SouthPark and find you handsome guys some new swag." She ushered the group back into the van. It was fun watching them decide what they wanted this year. Cheydon went straight for the basketball jersey of his favorite player. "Does it cost too much, Kate?" "No, Chey, if this is the one you want, this is your gift. I can't wait to see you in it. The way you play, kids will be buying the jersey with your number on it someday."

Everett chose his favorite football team's sweatshirt. She bought the sweatpants for him too.

Declan loved lacrosse and she got him a new stick, not quite clothes, but she made the exception.

And Griffin chose a new pair of tennis shoes.

They were all so excited. It truly did feel better to her to watch their happiness, instead of buying something new for herself.

After that, they picked out presents for the kids they didn't know, but who didn't have a cousin or even parents that could buy gifts for them. She felt so proud of them as they selected the items they liked.

"Now, guys, let's go get some pizza. We are going to eat it in the van on the way to, well, on the way to somewhere before we go the hotel." There was a light show at the Charlotte Motor Speedway. She hadn't been to it for years, but remembered it as spectacular. She wanted to be there by six when they opened so they'd have plenty of time afterwards for the game room and the pool at the hotel.

They arrived at the speedway and the boys seemed to enjoy it. "Guys, isn't it amazing? Over four million lights! You and your dad do a great job at your house, but this is over the top, huh?" They liked it, although Chey spent lots of time on his phone. Well, he was sixteen after all.

She made a note to come back again next year, even allowed herself to imagine Dan coming with them.

On the way to the hotel Cheydon was texting furiously with some-one. Kate wondered who it could be, but knew her sixteen-year-old cousin would want his privacy. Once they were in the hotel lobby, she found out who it was. "Dan, what are you doing here?" she asked but her tone of voice and smile showed her pleasure.

He and Chey held up their phones displaying their texts, grinning as they did.

"I hope you don't mind," Dan said, "But I bought an extra room so a couple of the boys can sleep in my room if they'd like and you can all have more room."

"I don't mind at all; do you guys want to hang out at the pool now?" They were definitely ready and the group went to change into swimwear. She was glad Dan had joined them. They had so much fun rough-housing in the pool and competing with him in the game room. And it gave her a chance to see him interact with kids. The two older boys wanted to spend the night with him, something about a guy movie. She and Declan and Griffin fell asleep to the tv as well, and joined the others for room service in the morning. They flipped the pairings and the two youngest boys rode back to Beacon with him. Chey and Everett told her on the way home that they thought he was cool. They were only six and four the last time they had spent any time with Dan.

The rest of Friday found Dan busy preparing for the dinner he was hosting. All his friends had done so much he wanted to thank them in the best way he knew how. Mike and Julie would be there too and their restaurant had always been an inspiration to him. He wanted them to enjoy the meal and the camaraderie. It looked like it was going to be a full house. Kate went there right after dropping off Cheydon and Everett so she could help him; he'd also hired three of the employees he was borrowing from the Riggio's to cook and serve. Not having cooked for many of his friends yet, he was both anxious and excited to do so. He hoped it would go over as well as the hot chocolate flights had on Winter Stroll.

"I'll do cleanup as we go and help serve tonight," Kate offered. Not much of a cook herself, she thought that would keep her busy and she could keep the kitchen running smoothly.

"What about all those culinary skills?" he asked jokingly. She laughed in return but stuck with cleanup duty. Yoga had taught her the meditative value, not only of doing simple tasks, but also doing them with a present, quiet mind. It always made her think of her favorite scripture, 'Be still and know.' When she was younger, she would have thought spending the day in a café washing dishes sounded like failure, like she wasn't important enough. She knew the opposite now to be true. Maybe it sounded cheesy, but what she did didn't matter to her as much as how she did it. And who she was with.

As the rest of them busied themselves with chopping vegetables, making homemade sauces and rolls, preparing the chicken crust, baking pies, Kate found herself enjoying the light banter, laughter, ooh, and the aroma. Did anything smell better than pumpkin pie?

Expecting at least thirty guests, most of the tables held four people, so there would be seven or eight tables for her to serve tonight. She was slightly nervous because it was way out of her comfort zone, made a little easier because she was friends or family with everyone coming tonight. Absolutely nothing to worry about. It bothered her a little that it looked like the place that it would be during regular hours. She thought it was probably just her being a girl, but the only special touch they really had was the pretty centerpieces.

Much to her surprise and delight, others had that same thought and were providing a beautiful solution. Her Aunt Ali showed up with a basketful of linens. She had been acquiring antique tablecloths over the years and had amassed quite the collection. Here she was generously offering them to Dan for the night. Now it would look more like a charming little bistro.

An hour later, her friend Tammy came with boxes, literally boxes of antique dishes to share for the evening. Mismatched and therefore just the right look to create interesting tablescapes. She hugged her good friend as they both stood back and admired the lovely effect. The cafe had truly been transformed. She called out to Dan, "Come look at this if you can spare a minute." The look on his face said it all. Good thing too because all he could say was, "wow!" Then a spontaneous hug that wrapped up both women, even though he barely knew Tammy. They all laughed with joy and relief at the ordinary moment that felt extraordinary.

And two hours later the guests began to arrive. Kate tried out her hostessing skills, which really weren't any different from greeting yogis at her studio. She wanted everyone to relax and offered hot apple cider or champagne to friends as they shed their coats and hung them on the hall trees. "Choose any table that is to your liking," she suggested. "Sit with old friends or mingle with new." And to her great pleasure, she noticed that many chose to mix it up.

Chris and Jenny would normally sit with Amy and Andy. They chose the Riggio's as their dining companions. Maggie sat with the other singles, Shanti and Dan's friend Joe. Jack was the fourth, rounding out the group. She wondered if her mom had invited him. Maggie was keeping unusually mum when it came to the new doctor. Kate was still itching to know more about him.

Before they knew it, everyone was enjoying both the company of friends old and new, and sampling hors d'oeuvres. Laughter and escalated voices filled the air and muffled the Christmas music playing softly in the background. The pepper jelly on cream cheese seemed to be a fast favorite and that delighted Kate; it was her favorite as well.

Dan and his kitchen help soon announced to the group it was time to take their seats, and that dinner would be served by the lovely waitress/hostess Kate. Once the expected giggles and guffaws died down, Kate brought out the warm rolls, butter, and spinach salads which were quickly and happily devoured. Following salad, came the pecan crusted chicken and rosemary roasted red potatoes. The diners practically licked their plates clean, but still found room to finish off their meals with pumpkin pie and Dan's homemade whipped cream.

Applause erupted when Dan and the other chefs came out to take a bow. The evening had been a wild success. And he was grateful for the opportunity to gift his friends with the special event. Dan stopped over at Maggie, Jack, Shanti and Joe's table to see how the singles were faring. And it appeared to him that there might just be a little bit more spark between Joe and Shanti than Joe had shared. Wouldn't that be something!

Most everyone lingered, not in any hurry to leave. Once Kate and Dan made it back to her place, Freddie greeted them; they could tell he was eager for an evening walk. But no such luck tonight. They were exhausted. Kate started a fire. Dan made them some decaf and they snuggled together on the living room couch, Freddie between them. The next thing they knew, sun was shining through the window slats.

RECIPES

Pecan crusted chicken

- 1 ½ pounds skinless boneless chicken breasts

- 2 c. pecan halves

- 3 level T flour

- 1 t salt

- ½ t black pepper

- ½ t paprika

- ½ t onion powder

- ½ t garlic powder

- 2 large eggs

Directions

- Preheat oven to 400 degrees

- Line large baking sheet with parchment paper

- Pound chicken breasts thin and cut into strips

- Pulse ½ c pecan halves in food processor or blender until fine crumbs

- Mix fine crumbs with flour, salt, pepper, paprika, onion and garlic powder

- Pulse rest of pecan halves into larger coarse pieces

- Whisk eggs.

- Coat each chicken strip in the pecan/flour mixture

- Dip in egg

- Shake off excess and then roll in coarse pieces

- Place on baking sheet

- Bake for 10 minutes

- Turn each piece over

- Bake 10 minutes more

- Check that they are baked through

- Serve with your favorite condiment. (honey mustard is great)

Spinach salad

- Dressing

- 1 medium lemon

- 2 T white wine vinegar

- ¼ c sugar

- 1 T olive oil

- 2 t poppy seeds

Directions:

- Juice lemon

- Combine all ingredients and whisk

Salad

- ½ c sliced almonds
- 1 c strawberries, sliced
- 1 large apple, sliced
- 1/3 small red onion, sliced
- ½ c crumbled feta
- 1 pkg baby spinach

Directions:

- Combine ingredients except almonds
- Sprinkle almonds on top
- Pour dressing over and mix gently
- Serve immediately

Chapter 17

Once they woke up and got over the somewhat-awkward-yet-kind-of-wonderful morning, while they sipped their morning coffee, Kate reminded Dan that they were babysitting for the Spring boys that evening. Dan was definitely on board, both to hang out with the kids and to spend time with her. But he had never spent much time around little kids and since he and Kate were both only children, he wondered how they'd do. Hopefully she had babysat before because he never had, except for yesterday of course, but those boys were older and lots of fun. It did help that he knew Adam and Tyler were great kids.

They were both tired after the past couple of days and wanted to take it easy today before gearing up to face the daunting task of babysitting; they allowed themselves a break and spent the day not doing much more than reading by the fireplace. By the time they got to their friends' house they felt ready to take care of the boys. No plans but to wing it. How hard could it be, he wondered. Chris and Jenny did it every day, after all. And Kate had so much experience spending time with her cousins, she wasn't nervous about taking care of these little guys. She knew them so well.

Chris welcomed them and went over a few details while they waited for Jenny to come downstairs. They would be fine, he assured them. The boys had already eaten dinner and if they wanted, maybe they could decorate Christmas cookies with them. Jenny had already baked three dozen cookies. They were stored in a tin on the counter. No worries if they didn't want to. But they pounced on the idea. It would be a fun activity, maybe a little messy, but fun.

Just then Jenny and the boys came downstairs. The boys were excited to see Kate and Dan; they ran downstairs, practically knocking their mom over on the way. "Whoa boys, mom doesn't walk that well in heels as it is. Careful!" she shrieked. Chris let out a wolf whistle, his go-to for letting Jenny know she looked beautiful. Kate and Dan agreed. Dan told her she "cleaned up well," his idea of an appropriate compliment.

Kate admired her friend's style. She'd styled her long blond hair in a French twist and inserted a small holly leaf in the top. Classy and festive. She wore a black jersey off the shoulder jumpsuit and strappy black heels. Jenny had maintained her thin figure after having both boys and looked stunning. Kate told her as much.

"Gosh, thanks y'all. You sure do know how to make a girl feel special."

While Chris helped her into her coat, she hugged and kissed both boys and told them to be good. And they were off.

"Have fun!" Kate and Dan yelled out the door.

They asked Adam and Tyler what they wanted to do. Play a game, play with their toys, or decorate the Christmas cookies? The boys ran to the kitchen and reached for the cookie tin. "Cookies for the win," Dan hurried in and dove just in time to save the tin from crashing to the floor. Kate lined up all the frosting and sprinkles on the kitchen table and the four of them began. Adam and Tyler were having a blast. Cookies were covered in frosting and sprinkles twice as thick as the cookies themselves. As soon as they finished decorating a few, the boys became far more interested in sampling their creations. Who's kidding whom? The boys and the babysitters alike. Soon the two that were supposed to be in charge realized they'd better put a stop to that or they would have hyped up sugar monsters on their hands.

"Ok, bath time for you, cookie monsters." Dan scooped up the boys like he was carrying footballs under each arm and ran them up to the bathtub, while Kate cleared the kitchen mess. By the time she joined them upstairs the boys were in their footie pajamas and had snuggled in beside Dan for a bedtime story. As she stood in the doorway, she couldn't help smiling at the picture the three of them made. Dan had bathed and dressed them. He was a pro at this.

Three story books later, the boys were tucked into their beds fast asleep. Kate and Dan plopped on the couch. "I think that went well," Dan offered.

Kate nodded in agreement. "Did I ever tell you about how Andy and I decorated cookies every year from kindergarten on through elementary school? I'm going to have to dig out the pictures, especially the ones from that first year. My mom bought a snowman mold and we would each decorate three big cookies, so loaded with candy that we probably used a large bag full on top of the thick frosting we layered on each cookie."

She couldn't help but think what a natural Dan had been with the boys; her thoughts jumped ahead to what kind of dad he would be, if he ever even wanted kids. She was deep in the rabbit hole of future possibilities when he nudged her. Dan looked playfully at Kate, "What's on your mind?" She couldn't tell him. Or could she? Slowly she tiptoed into the shallow water of what she hoped was their future.

"You looked like a natural with the boys. Were you having as much fun as it looked like you were?"

He nodded, "surprised me how much fun it was. Chris and Jenny are good parents. The boys are well behaved."

"And happy," she agreed.

She changed the subject and cautiously asked him to tell her about his life in New York.

He cringed and hesitated, not really wanting to relive that part of his life, especially with her.

"I'm glad that's the past and this is my life now."

"Was your life big city glamorous?" she joked. All she had to go on were novels she'd read, movies set in the Big Apple. She imagined fast paced life, exciting work---

"Not at all." He told her it was work, work, and more work. Work to get ahead, too cutthroat for him. Dog eat dog kind of feeling. Not that there wasn't some value in the work and also some good people with solid integrity, but it just wasn't the life he wanted. And the congestion of the city often made him feel hemmed in.

"Sometimes I think people want to move to New York because of the unrealistic picture that tv and movies often paint of the way they live. Do you remember the apartment on 'Friends' that the girls lived in? That place was spacious compared to mine. This couch to the fireplace? Not much roomier than that."

"More often than not," he shared, "I felt that ugly tightness in my chest that indicated to me that I needed to take a different path. I've always had a dream to own a café and I started wondering what it would be like to settle down here. I wasn't about to be able to afford the rent on a café in the city." She quietly wondered what his relationship with his old girlfriend was like, but she didn't want to let her into the lives they had now. She told herself that she didn't need to know. Not really. That was his past and she wanted to be his future. He didn't bring it up either. They sat and watched one of their favorite Christmas movies as it played on tv.

After the movie ended, Dan realized he had been trying to tell her about Belinda for days and he had the opportunity tonight and blew it. Now was as good a time as any.

"Kate, there is something I have wanted to bring up…" He was interrupted as Chris and Jenny opened the front door.

"Fun night? "Kate queried.

"Ours was great," Jenny replied, "but yours with the boys…were they good?"

Kate drew their attention to the frosted cookies. "They're cookie artists!" She told them that the boys wanted them to enjoy one when they got home. So, the four of them complied, happily ending the night with cookies and hot chocolate. Dan and Kate filled them in on the boys' evening and remarked what great parents they were.

The old friends reminisced about Christmas parties they'd all enjoyed in high school together and shared more than a few laughs.

"Remember the time we went ice skating?" Kate asked the gang. They had gone to an indoor rink in Charlotte and only Jenny and Andy had ever skated before. The rest of them were a mess on ice, but no one left with any sustained injuries. They weren't sure how. They were all so awkward that the experienced skaters at the rink were doing everything imaginable to avoid them, but they were the ones that usually fell. Collateral damage.

"Do you guys remember that even though I was more like a sister to Andy, when we skated together, Amy was jealous? I couldn't believe it. It sure wasn't my intention!"

Chris looked at her in disbelief.

"What?" she asked him, her green eyes big.

"Amy, jealous? I wanted to wring Andy's neck!"

"No way. I never knew. That's really sweet."

"And hilarious," Dan chimed in.

Chapter 18

Sunday morning Kate awoke to thoughts swirling around in her head of all they needed to do at Dan's place before he hosted the caroling after party. She was a little surprised he had offered to host since he was a newcomer to the tradition, but was also pretty sure that he'd wanted his friends to see the house. He had jumped back into life in Beacon with both feet. She got to thinking that he didn't even have a Christmas tree. They'd have to fix that. Cannot have a Christmas party without a tree. Maybe he would want to cut down one. Not too far out of town there was a tree farm where they could choose one and cut it down themselves. She usually had her tree up by now, but hers would have to wait. Getting his place ready needed to be job one.

After getting out for a quick run with Freddie, she impulsively decided to grab a couple of steaming hot hazelnut coffees at the village coffee shop. She took Freddie and the coffees to Dan's place without even calling ahead, hoping he wouldn't mind. She found him walking around the yard and handed him one of the coffees. "What in the world are you doing here so early, whoa, and with coffee?" he asked.

"I was just about to ask you why you're wandering aimlessly around in your yard."

"Not aimless, aimful. I'm thinking there has to be a perfect Christmas tree in this wilderness," he told her.

"That's what I was coming over to talk to you about. But I was thinking about going to the tree farm. Why not see if there's one here instead? I'm glad I wore my boots. It's a mess out here for sure. If you find one, how are you planning to cut it down?"

"You'd be surprised at the old tools in the garage. I unearthed a hand saw that'll get the job done," he told her, looking like an excited little boy on Christmas morning. This home was the perfect purchase for him.

Tromping around through the underbrush, they searched his acre lot. Nothing was looking like it could do the trick until they spotted a seven feet tall spruce tree that they would have chosen in a tree lot. Almost simultaneously the two pointed, "that one!" they both exclaimed.

Laughing at the unanimous decision, Kate stepped out of the way while Dan worked the saw.

After that the hardest part was dragging it through the tangled mess of a yard to the front porch.

"I'm thinking the far corner of the living room, but I have to clean it up before we bring it in," Dan remarked.

"You don't have to clean it alone. That's why I'm here. What if we scrub down the hall bathroom too? Those two rooms are all you need to have ready for Friday night."

"That sounds like a plan to me. And you don't have to pitch in, but I'm grateful you want to."

They needed breakfast before putting in that kind of work so he baked a batch of his cranberry walnut granola and they ate it with sliced bananas and almond milk. The smell of it was so enticing. She hadn't realized how hungry she was. Digging in, she complimented him, "I could eat this every day, Dan. Maybe I will when you open for breakfast."

"I could too, he agreed," and don't think you'll ever have to buy it at the cafe," he assured her. "With everything you are doing to help me out, you'll eat there free for life."

"Oh, I can get behind that plan."

Energized again, they walked around the corner of the kitchen, through the dining room and across the front of the house to the spacious living room. She stood in the doorway with him and took it all in, thinking about where they should start and also where all the furniture would be placed, once they found furniture. The couch and bar were the only things remaining in the dusty room. To the left, large windows flanked the side of the room that ran across the front of the house; across from where they stood, two unpainted oak roomy bookcases framed either side of the fireplace. The oak mantle was original, simple and unadorned. Windows over each bookcase let in light, or at least they would once they were cleaned, and once the outside ivy covering them was cleared. The wall along the back side of the house held the bar and they would use that to serve snacks on Friday night. They stood in the wide entry, silently deciding what they thought about the condition of the floor. Also made of oak and unpainted, it looked to them to be in fairly good shape.

Kate offered a couple of ideas. "I'm thinking we work top down, sweep the cobwebs from the ceiling, clean the windows and wipe down the bookcases, fireplace and bar, then start scrubbing the floor."

"I'm ready if you are. Want to go to your place and grab the cleaning supplies that you have at home, and I'll head to the hardware store for brooms, buckets, and sponges?"

"Let's make a list and split the stuff you need to buy and what I can grab from home," she suggested and they ventured back into the kitchen to sit down and make a plan.

By the time they gathered the necessary cleaning supplies and tackled the living room, the sun was setting and the room was starting to look presentable. More would have to be done before it could ever serve as the room for B&B guests to enjoy, but for their good friends on Friday night it would work. They still needed to clean up the leather couch that had he inherited with the house. And they would set up the Christmas tree in the corner right in front of the window, between the fireplace wall and the bar wall, decorate it simply and fill it with as many strands of white lights as they could manage. Kate wished he had ornaments.

They needed more furniture by Friday. Kate thought they maybe could hit up the nearby furniture outlet for starters; the place was in a huge warehouse, at least the size of five football fields laid end to end. No place like North Carolina for furniture hunting.

"Maybe we could go shopping for some items tomorrow for a couple hours, or how is Tuesday? My teaching schedule is much lighter that day."

Dan thought Tuesday afternoon would be good and Kate promised she'd draw up a plan for furniture placement if he would like. She kind of fancied herself an amateur decorator.

"That would be really great; it's not my strength at all. I'm better off sticking to the kitchen," he admitted. Matter of fact, it won't be anything special, but I'm hungry if you are and I can make us a quick meal."

"Great, I'd like to stay in here and play with furnishing ideas anyway."

She grabbed a legal pad from his sunroom and sat down to plan, and before long had some ideas. They could place the couch across from the fireplace, and set a sizable coffee table between the two. A couple of smaller sofas could face each other, creating a "U" shape seating arrangement. That way there would be plenty of comfortable seating in front of the fireplace where their friends would sit and talk this Friday night and eventually guests would enjoy when the place opened. He'd want six barstools at the bar and a couple of easy chairs under the front windows with a little table or chest in between where drinks could be placed and a lamp to provide light for reading. A nice big area rug would make it all more comfortable. That ought to be enough for this week and Dan could always add more furnishings in time.

Dan called out that dinner was ready and she made her way into the kitchen.

"Smells so good," she said taking a seat. "Mexican, I love it." He turned to face her as he pulled the pan out of the oven, and she giggled at the silly feminine apron he'd found in one of the kitchen drawers. He kept a straight face, "I remembered that you liked enchiladas so I just threw together some simple ones."

"Yum, they don't taste simple and I'm glad you're comfortable flaunting your feminine side. Wish I had my phone handy to snap a picture of you in that apron," she grinned.

So good. She greedily devoured them. They both did.

The day had been tiring but they felt a sense of accomplishment.

RECIPE

Easy Cheesy Enchiladas

(I have been making this recipe for at least 20 years. My family loves them and we enjoy them at least once a month. I often serve them for guests.)

- Preheat oven to 375 degrees.

- Grease a 9 by 13 pan.

- 3 T white or yellow onion chopped

- 2 T butter melted

- 8 oz cream cheese

- 1 t cumin

- 1 c. salsa

- 2 cans enchilada sauce, however spicy you like (I use medium)

- At least 4 cups of cheddar or Mexican blend cheese, separated into 2 c. each

- 8 large soft flour tortillas

- Sliced green onions

- Sour cream

- Jalapenos

- Black olives

- Avocados

- Sauté onion in melted butter about 5 minutes

- Add cream cheese, salsa and cumin and stir until cheese is melted.

- Pour a thin layer of enchilada sauce in the baking dish

Don't be surprised that this next step is messy:

- Dredge a tortilla in the sauce, add about 1/3 to ½ c of the cream cheese mixture into the tortilla, pile on a little cheddar and fold up the tortilla. Place it seam down in the baking dish and continue until all eight are in.

- Pour the rest of the enchilada sauce over and add the rest of the cheddar.

- Bake covered with foil for about 25 minutes, uncover until the cheese is melted.

- Add whatever you want of the green onions, sour cream, jalapenos and black olives, cilantro,

- avocados.

- Enjoy!

Chapter 19

Monday found Kate tied up teaching three yoga classes and Dan just as busy working in the café. Maggie and Kate went over details to create the best village holiday party ever, deciding to buy novelty holiday socks for all the guests since this year they were cohosting with Dan and they had a no footwear policy on their yoga studio floor. They giggled as they pictured their guests dressed in their finest, with goofy holiday socks adorning their feet. Everyone would look proper while in Dan's side of the event, then stash their shoes in cubbies while on their side. Hopefully all the partygoers would be good sports about it.

Later Kate had some free time; she started thinking about a color scheme for the furniture they were selecting for Dan's living room tomorrow. The brown leather couch he'd inherited with the house was worn but comfy and substantial in size. They needed a rug that would ground the room and provide a welcoming and inviting feel. Something in medium tones, neutral that could handle wear and tear, she kept trying to decide but thought it would be better just to go out and see what caught their eyes tomorrow. They'd also want to start filling the book shelves, not just with books, but also with puzzles and old standby board games. And they'd want baskets to hold firewood, blankets, and floor pillows to make the large room feel homey. She knew all of it could wait; technically he didn't need it all done now. He may not be open for months, but she found herself excited about the project and had a hard time holding back.

Friday night's caroling tradition was such a special one. The group had grown over the years to about twenty; some were couples that had been together since high school. Others moved back to town, bringing spouses they'd met in college or after, and they'd become a group Kate really enjoyed. She and Shanti were the only ones still single. This year it would be good to bring Dan back into the fold, and Shanti had invited Joe to join them.

Their former high school teachers loved it and made sure to stay home that Friday night to welcome the group of enthusiastic, if not always on-key, singers. She wanted the after party at Dan's to be wonderful; maybe that was why she was going overboard with the plans for his living room.

In the meantime, Dan was on his way to the old Riggio's restaurant site to see if any progress had been made since he saw them on Friday. His cell phone rang in his pocket and he let it go to voicemail. These days almost no one left messages. They just returned the call when it was convenient and sometimes played a little phone tag. In his opinion, it was better than retrieving long messages. But this caller left a message so he pulled out his phone to check it while strolling to Mike and Julie's place.

He stopped walking when he realized who had called. The message was from Belinda. He had hoped she was done calling, but no such luck. She said that his father had contacted her and told her he thought they still belonged together, and she was coming to Charlotte for work this week so maybe she'd drive down to Beacon. She was eager to see him. His face fell as he listened. The very last thing he wanted was to reconnect with her. Filled with anger towards his dad, he turned around and headed to see if he was at home. He wanted to confront him in person and hoped this time he could at least get him to stop trying to control his life. He'd succumbed to his pressure when he was younger. He wasn't ever going to put up with it again.

Of course, he wasn't home, but Dan left a voice mail of his own for once and told his dad in no uncertain terms to leave his personal life to him. Then, realizing that he had no other option but to reply, he left Belinda a message that was curt and pointed in tone and content. He let her know that his father was completely off base and she need not make the visit to Beacon. He wished her well, but he had moved on. Now he was in no mood to see anyone. Kate would see through any attempt he made to be lighthearted so he was a little relieved when she called to say she was looking forward to furniture shopping tomorrow, but tonight she had a tradition she planned to keep with her girlfriends. She got a little sense that something was bothering him, but brushed it aside and assumed he was tired from all the work they'd put in yesterday.

Dan couldn't keep from thinking about all the decisions he had made in the past, seeking his dad's approval, and yes, even trying to win his love. Upon reflection he realized this was the way to build an authentic life. How good he felt in his own skin now, making decisions based on what he wanted. If only he could get the nagging thought of Belinda possibly showing up in Beacon out of his mind. As forward as she was, he couldn't imagine she was that pushy. She had once been so attractive to him. Now he didn't find her desirable in any way. It really was amazing. When you change the way you look at things, the things and people you look at change, and the person he wanted to look at, be with, was Kate. He knew deep down that he should probably tell her the whole story but he didn't want to mess with what they had.

Chapter 20

Kate was hosting Amy, Shanti and Jenny tonight for a tradition they had enjoyed over the past few years. As far back as high school the four of them got together every week during the tv season of 'A Perfect Match,' a dating show where an eligible bachelor got to know and date several women who were vying for his love. These days they only watched the finale together since their lives were so much more complicated with two of them having families of their own and the other two busy with their careers.

Kate had set out wine, cheese, crackers and chocolate, the four party food groups in her opinion. One by one her friends arrived and they gathered around the television to enjoy watching and critiquing the finale as the bachelor made his final decision, choosing one woman to either continue dating or, so much more exciting as a finale, to propose. Kate and her besties had a pool going throughout the season, each one had a "team" of five women they had drafted as their picks to win his heart, much like guys did with fantasy football. This season Shanti and Amy still had women from their teams in the finale, adding to the fun.

As the show progressed, the four friends started discussing the events of the season.

"Do you guys think he looks like Dan?" Amy asked. "All season long he has reminded me of him."

"Now that you mention it, maybe he does a little," Kate said as she took a sip of wine. I wonder if that's why I enjoyed this season so much. I hadn't really made the connection."

Shanti chimed in, "That's weird, Kate, kind of a subliminal attraction, huh?"

"I think it's his smile," Jenny said.

"Speaking of Dan," Shanti was wondering, and buoyed by the wine asked, "What's going on Kate? Now that he's buying the B&B and the café, looks to me like he's ready to settle down with a certain old flame of his own," she teased.

Kate didn't say anything right away. If only she herself knew what the answer to that was. She sure didn't need him breaking her heart again, especially since he would be living in the same small town with her, and working right next door. And to add to the concern, he'd seemed off lately, quiet and bothered by something. She grabbed some chocolate and refocused on the show.

"Well, think of it," Amy answered Shanti like Kate wasn't even there. "He's always been a business minded guy. He may just be throwing his focus on the businesses here, happy to be with Kate as a friend, a good friend. I just wonder."

Jenny piped in, "No, I think he is totally in love with Kate, not just coming back here for business."

Kate couldn't take the banter any longer. She was already worried about the way Dan seemed distant. Something was bothering him. She could tell.

"Ladies, please!" She sounded angry with them. "We are over here to see what happens on this finale. And you are all acting like Dan and I are the characters on the show. This isn't some kind of episode we are watching. This is my life!"

The four had always squabbled like sisters, and they were quick to forgive each other.

All three friends turned to her, sorry they had turned it into something about Kate.

"I'm so sorry, Kate. I started it with my silly comment," Shanti said. "I think I let the wine loosen my inhibitions about discussing your personal life."

"No, Kate," Amy said, "It's not Shanti's fault, it's mine. I was talking about your life like it was the tv show we were watching. I'm sorry."

"Ok, I probably over reacted to the whole conversation," Kate remarked. "It's just that Dan has been a little distant lately and I'm worried."

They all refocused on the program, and Kate tried to let it go, without much success.

Tuesday afternoon when Dan picked her up, he still seemed a little distracted, but she chalked it up to preoccupation about all the furniture they needed to find.

Arriving at the outlet, she asked, "What do you say we look for a large area rug first to ground the room and give us a sense of colors you want?"

"Lead the way. Sounds good to me. I'm glad you know what you're doing."

Hundreds of rugs were stacked in the room. And they pulled out a few of them that drew their eyes. They chose a thick neutral, comfortable rug with muted browns in a simple geometric pattern.

Next, they selected six barstools that looked comfortable and sturdy, with brown leather seats that would be easy to wipe down. Metal frames provided a nice contrast to all the wood in the room, and they selected a couple really comfortable blue easy chairs for the quiet reading area.

Two small couches with beige slipcovers that could easily be removed and washed would be perfect as well.

"Let's have these delivered and see how things are looking for the time being," Dan decided. "I may have to reload the wallet before I get any more." He was starting to think that he needed to nail down the partnership with Jack if he wanted to get the place open by summer.

They were relieved to learn that all of it could be delivered on Thursday since they didn't want to host Friday night on the bare floor. They grabbed a pizza on the way home to enjoy while putting up the Christmas tree they had cut down on Sunday.

"Kate, I've been wanting to get your opinion on an offer that I am thinking about accepting,"

"What's that?"

"Jack Smith offered to help me finance the place by becoming a silent partner."

"That might just be amazing, Dan. What are you going to do?"

"Well, since I want to be open by next summer and my resources aren't exactly unlimited, I think he seems like a good person to go into business with. I'm considering sitting down with him. The way your mom has taken to him helps me to lean that direction. She is such a grounded good judge of character."

"Can't hurt to talk to him, might be just the thing," she agreed.

"Doesn't it look divine in this corner, Dan?" Kate admired the way the tree lights reflected in the corner window. They stood arm in arm, admiring the simple beauty of the tree giving off the only lighting in the room. The darkened room glowed captivatingly as the white lights twinkled softly. She was content, she realized, happier than she'd been in a long time. It was starting to feel like it might be too good to be true. He, on the other hand, was worried about Belinda actually having the nerve to maybe show up in Beacon in a few days. He couldn't shake the concern he felt.

And he didn't want to ruin the magical moment for Kate so he tried to push the thought aside once more.

The next two days ushered in a whirlwind of preparations for the caroling night, the living room setup, more work in the café, Kate's schedule at the studio, and holiday shopping on top of it all. They went by in a blur. Kate had even hit up some resale shops and used bookstores to start filling in the bookshelves.

Her favorite shops were only about twenty miles away out on Highway 74. She borrowed Aunt Ali's van again on Wednesday and drove out on the winding country roads to the shops with the intention of finding the right accents to warm up the room. She didn't have any idea of what Dan would want for Christmas, and she figured sprucing up the living room would be the perfect present this year.

She first went into the shop that housed good books in the back corner booth. So many of her favorite authors were represented and before she knew it, she had stacks of novels filling her shopping cart with books by Sparks, Brown, Hale, Thayer, Macomber, Grisham, Follett, Archer, and more. She wanted Dan to be able to offer them to guests to take with them if they weren't finished, maybe leave one of their own to keep the library fresh.

She also picked up puzzles, baskets to store firewood next to the fireplace, throw pillows with quilted fronts, flannel fabric, floral prints, any one that caught her eye, along with a few cozy throws. These were the touches that would make the room. Dan texted:

What's up?

Christmas shopping.

Free tonight for dinner?

Sure, what time?

Come by the café at six.

See you then.

She wondered what he was up to now.

By six, she arrived at his house with her car full of the day's purchases. It would be fun shelving the books and puzzles she'd found, but the pillows, throws, and baskets would have to wait until tomorrow when the furniture arrived. Since his place was just around the corner from the café, she parked there to unload the books and puzzles after dinner and switch cars back again with Ali.

The night was unseasonably warm so she walked to the café, unzipping her coat and enjoying the canopy of beautiful starry skies as she strolled over. As she rounded the corner, she saw the surprise he had planned for them. The outdoor dining heaters had arrived and he had a bistro table set up for the two of them outside in front of the café. White lights wrapped the door and windows and a large wreath hung in the center window. Luminaries were lined up along the front of the building. So incredibly beautiful. Dan was sitting outside with a bottle of red wine, two wine glasses and appetizers on the table. She was absolutely blown away by the setting and all the trouble he had gone to.

"I thought you might enjoy an outdoor picnic. Such nice weather for December," he said.

She smiled, "I think I just might. This is incredible." Christmas music was playing through his outdoor speakers. "I know it's early, but Merry Christmas from me to you. I figured you might like this better than a present."

"It's just perfect. Experiences are always better than things."

"Here, let me pour you a glass of wine."

"Cheers!" they toasted the ordinary Wednesday night.

The appetizer was simple, but he had made it for the party earlier and knew it was her favorite, a cream cheese block slightly softened and covered with hot pepper jelly, served on crackers. She ate it with abandon, and realized how hungry she was. She had skipped lunch and that was a rarity for her.

"Any luck shopping today?" he asked, topping his cracker with the cream cheese mixture.

"Actually, I have a few items in the car for the living room at the B&B. My early present to you."

"That was the shopping you were doing?"

"Sure was."

"Can't wait to see what you got! I wouldn't know where to start."

"It's kind of my thing, so I'm glad you don't mind."

The timer went off on his phone, letting him know the main course was ready.

"Be right back."

After he went back inside, shoppers strolling the village stopped to ask her if the café was open already. She happily explained that tonight was a private party, but it would be opening soon.

He brought out dinner, a flatbread pizza he had concocted with mozzarella, parmesan, pears, and topped with arugula and spinach. They drizzled his homemade ranch dressing over it. So good.

Dessert was Italian wine cake with decaf coffee. What better gift than a man who wanted to cook for her and serve it in such a special setting. She told him so. He just smiled. And blushed. She could see his cheeks redden even though they were outside in the dark.

Kate helped Dan clean up and they walked back to her aunt and uncle's van to get out what she had purchased today. She wished she'd had her phone ready to take a video of his reaction.

"Did you hold up a library?" He quizzed her.

She smirked and replied, "Maybe. I'll never tell. We have to get all this inside so I can at least return the van."

"Let's get it done then. You're crazy, you know that?" But the look on his face said he liked her kind of crazy. Kate thought maybe things were looking up again on this roller coaster ride she was on.

RECIPES

Flatbread pizza

- Slather store bought flatbread with olive oil, sprinkle with salt and pepper.

- Cover liberally with mozzarella and sliced pears.

- Bake according to flatbread directions and check until crust is brown and cheese is melted.

- Remove from oven and top with arugula and spinach.

- We drizzle ranch dressing on top and add parmesan.

Italian wine cake (even better for a couple of days after)

- Preheat oven to 350 degrees

- Grease and flour a bundt pan

- 1 pkg yellow cake mix

- A five oz package instant vanilla pudding

- 1/3 c water

- 1/2 c vegetable oil

- Four large eggs

- 1/2 c red wine

Directions

- Stir cake mix and pudding mix together and add wet ingredients. Mix on low speed, then beat five more minutes on medium.

- Pour into pan and bake 40 minutes or until toothpick comes out clean when testing

- Glaze

- ½ c butter

- ½ c white sugar

- 1/2 c wine or water

- Heat until butter is melted and sugar is dissolved.

- Pour over warm cake.

Chapter 21

The furniture was delivered on Thursday afternoon. Kate had spent the better part of the morning arranging the bookshelves. Dan still couldn't get over how much she had bought. Once the furniture was placed and she added the pillows and throws the room looked inviting, she had to admit. They could fill the baskets with firewood later.

Friday morning found them touching up the details so he would feel proud to host the gang after caroling. She was excited to reveal the results of their hard work, but again she found Dan unusually reticent. He had seemed fine Wednesday night, but yesterday he seemed a little off again. It was starting to bother her. She had a nagging suspicion that something was on his mind. Well, he would open up about it when he was ready; she hoped so anyway.

At six that evening when everyone started arriving, the skies were clear and the temperature was around forty degrees, cold enough for caroling to be fun but not so cold that they'd be miserable outdoors. Some years had been unseasonably cold and others were so warm that it didn't have a Christmassy feeling. This weather was just right. Kate ushered the women in the back door to refrigerate or set out the goodies they'd brought for later. She didn't want to take them into the living room until they arrived back and she and Dan would have a chance to light some candles, start a fire in the fireplace and plug in the tree. Dan and the guys were outside deciding which cars to pile into to drive around to their former teachers' homes. Everyone looked festive decked out in their red and green sweaters, light winter coats, and the occasional stocking hat or scarf. Joe even brought a stash of Santa hats for anyone who needed a holiday hat to wear.

The Christmas tree was well lit, but otherwise unadorned so Kate had asked their friends to surprise Dan and to bring any old ornaments that had been lying around in the bottom of their ornament bins. She had a few of her own and figured they might have some as well. They had surprised her by not only bringing ornaments, but also cranberry ropes, popcorn chains, so much that she wasn't sure they could get it all on the tree. How much fun it was going to be to surprise Dan when they came back after singing. She had remembered that he didn't ever really have a tree after his mom died, and she also had loved seeing him decorating the tree at her mom's.

Their retired teachers looked forward to the event each year and as the group traveled from house to house, they were invited in for hot apple cider or offered cookies at some houses, savory treats at others. Merriment filled the night as they blared out the carols, laughing at some off-key notes. Every year was pretty much the same and that was one of the reasons they treasured the time together. Nothing felt better than giving back to the teachers that had given so much to them.

The highlight was always their last stop when they got to Mr. Adamson's, their former music teacher's home. His wife made a big batch of glogg, an irresistible spiked mulled cider and they gathered around Mr. Adamson as he accompanied them on the piano. The most fun was singing 'O Holy Night' as they literally fell on their knee caps every single year when they got to that part of the song. "Fall on your knees" they belted out and couldn't keep straight faces. Really cheesy and so much fun.

When they returned to the future B&B, Dan ushered the guys into the kitchen to reheat or unwrap what they'd brought and the women gathered the wood together to light a fire in the fireplace. Finally, Dan and the guys took the dishes in and set it all up on the bar; everyone was together, excited to see what Kate and Dan had done with the living room. The outcome was enchanting, warm and inviting. As the food was set up on the bar, and drinks were served, they all got the sense of what a lovely experience guests would enjoy when Dan opened.

Kate closed her eyes and just listened for a moment. Sometimes when she was in a crowd, she just wanted to feel invisible and relish the sounds of happiness. When she opened her eyes, they landed on Joe and Shanti.

"Jenny, look, Joe and Shanti seem to be getting along well, and this party and this group of friends, it's just a wonderful feeling."

"Oh, Kate, Jenny agreed, "I'm feeling the same way about it all!"

Looking around at how comfortable and relaxed her friends were, Kate just knew the future was going to be simply wonderful for all of them.

As they had every year, it was time to exchange white elephant gifts; everyone brought a wrapped present worth less than ten dollars. The fun thing about it was that they each drew a number. Amy drew number '1' and went first. She grabbed a gift which turned out to be novelty holiday socks. She thought they'd be fun to wear to the village party since everyone had to wear socks while on the yoga studio side, although the way the game went, she'd probably be opening several packages. She was right about that. Shanti was up next and had the option of grabbing the socks or unwrapping something else. She gave Amy a grin and "stole" the socks. Funny how competitive we all are. Things we would ordinarily pass up in a store, but that someone else has, we want it. And we just have to have it. Makes the game fun and often hilarious. By the time the night was over Amy must have opened at least eight presents. Kate was the lucky recipient of the last number so she ended up with the socks.

Before the evening ended, Kate grabbed Chris, Andy and Joe to lug in the bins full of ornaments they had all gathered. Dan laughed as the group pitched in and decorated the tree. Everyone had a great time reminiscing, and Dan found himself thinking about all the years he had missed with this great group who treasured simple times filled with good company, good food. He'd been climbing the wrong ladder all these years. None of his downtime had been spent like this. He hadn't even allowed himself parties unless they were an advantageous way to advance in the business world. That was all in his past now.

Once Dan and Kate were alone, he brought up the offer Jack had made to become a silent partner.

"I talked to him this afternoon. I'm leaning toward accepting. I can just see how limited my funds will be on my own, and I want to do this right."

"OMG Dan that's fantastic. Sounds like something I'd go for if I were you. I have a good feeling about Jack."

"Me too. And I don't think we are alone in that."

Before he went to sleep that night, Dan started thinking about what he could do next with his own living space in the future. B&B. Talking with Jack about his interest in backing had given Dan the freedom to start making bigger plans, plans for when it wasn't just him living there.

They'd had such a good open conversation, about much more than finances. Dan had shared with Jack that he didn't think he should have to have backing, that he should be able to pull it off himself. That was his hesitation. Jack had replied that was one word that he had dropped from his vocabulary. 'Should.' In the past few years, through his yoga practice, he had come to learn that word was defeating at best. "Any time you say 'should,' stop and think about how futile it is and how limiting it can be." He had told him to see what happens when you remove it from your vocabulary for good. Dan reflected on it, and realized that was another way his dad had controlled him.

Done with the 'shoulds' in his life, he started thinking about possibilities instead. The space at the top of the back stairway, he could turn it into a master with a master bath. Once he created a private living area upstairs, he could use the two rooms he was now occupying as space for guests. After adding the upstairs master, he'd add a nicer bath so the one downstairs could serve the guests in the two back downstairs rooms. Those spaces would go to people who didn't mind walking through the kitchen area to their rooms. They'd be the lucky ones anyway. The coffee and snacks would be easy to grab late night or early morning. Those easygoing guests would be the most fun to house.

Across the hall from the master was a nice bedroom that could be a study or maybe, long term, a nursery. Or maybe, they should be downstairs with the guests all upstairs. He let himself go there. Thinking about a nursery. Drink that in. Yikes, he was getting way ahead of himself. But hey, a guy could dream.

Chapter 22

Kate slept in late the next morning. She only had to teach one class at noon, then meet with her mom and Dan to go over final details for the village party. The highlight of the meeting was finding out what a generous check they would be presenting on Christmas Eve to Julie and Mike Riggio. The giftwrapping fundraiser and proceeds from all the other village businesses added up to an amount beyond what they had imagined they could raise.

Outside they watched the company they had hired construct a covered walkway between the two businesses to better facilitate foot traffic during the party. A red carpet had been laid on the sidewalk to add to the festive atmosphere. And they had set up the kind of heaters restaurants use to heat outdoor dining areas along with the one Dan already had, so it would be more comfortable when they had to briefly go outside. Tammy covered the outdoors with ivy and string upon string of twinkling white lights and extended the decorations to include the walkway as well. She would decorate the yoga studio on Tuesday so classes could still be held until then.

The band would also set up on Tuesday in a corner of the studio and tables and chairs would be scattered throughout as well. Everything was falling into place.

Sunday morning was the day they had designated for Kate to finally get her own Christmas tree. She couldn't remember a year when her house hadn't been decorated by now. But there had been so much more happening this year. She hadn't minded the wait.

Dan picked up her and Freddie so they could drive to the tree farm a few miles out of town. The winding drive on pine tree lined country roads was peaceful and Kate found herself relaxed and enjoying the quiet. As she glanced out the window, she could hardly believe it.

"Dan," she exclaimed, "I think it's starting to snow!" Sure enough, those were tiny wet magical snowflakes hitting the windshield.

"Oh, I hope it doesn't melt before we get to the tree farm," she mused. "I just love it when we get a little snow. You must have found it beautiful it in the big city when it was deep in snow as you picked out your tree."

"The tree lots were just lined up on city sidewalks and more often than not the snow was crusty piles of dark gray slush. It wasn't the romantic scene you watch in movies," he frowned.

"Well. that sounds gross. I hope the trees are covered when we get there to pick out mine!"

And as if on cue, as they pulled up to the tree farm, her wish was granted. The trees were lovely, their branches covered in pristine fluffy white snow. "I'm glad we wore our boots," she cried out, she couldn't get to the trees fast enough, dashing around with childlike joy, happy to be able to run on her ankle again and invigorated by the unexpected snowfall. He laughed as he tried to catch up with her. Freddie was practically sprawled out on his belly sliding around on the cold snow.

"Look, "she ran to a pretty Douglas fir. "This is the one."

"You sure? There are plenty more to choose from."

"I'm sure. It's exactly right for my living room. When Jenny and Chris come tomorrow night, it will be so much fun to decorate it with the three of you."

She was starting to feel like this was going to be the best Christmas ever.

As she looked up at Dan through her snow-covered lashes, she almost had to pinch herself that he was back in her life. Her feelings for him could not be stronger and she was starting to believe he actually felt the same for her. He leaned in, she closed her eyes, and they started to...

Freddie ran between them, almost knocking them to their knees. Moment over.

She offered, "I'll cut down this one since you did the work at your place."

He was impressed as she cut it down and they flagged an attendant who would wrap it up and secure it atop the car.

"Brrr." Dan suggested, "Let's go inside while we wait and grab a hot apple cider." They tied Freddie to the porch and went inside.

By the time they drove back to her place the snow had stopped falling. But it had fallen long enough to give her a happy memory. They dragged the tree to her front porch and left it in a corner while they started stringing icicle lights on the porch railings. She pulled some of the boxwood wreaths from the trunk of the car and began hanging them by attaching wide flannel red and green plaid ribbon and decorating the two front windows and front door with the greenery. As they finished decking out the front porch Kate offered, "Let me make you lunch for once."

"Sounds great. I'll be in as soon as I can. And I'll grab the tree holder out of the garage to set your tree up for you."

Now inside the kitchen she wondered what she could pull together for lunch. She certainly wasn't the chef that he was. And they needed something warm for lunch today. She scanned the cupboards and fridge and found she had enough to pull together a minestrone. That was the one thing for which she always tried to keep ingredients on hand. She could eat it for days and it tasted better every day as the flavors melded together.

There was even a bakery loaf of French bread in the freezer. She pulled it out to thaw on the counter.

Chopping the vegetables as a Christmas movie played in the background on her kitchen tv, Kate was happy to be cooking for him. Her mom had made this recipe for as long as Kate could remember and it was one of probably a handful of recipes she had memorized. She was making a double batch so they could have it again tomorrow night when the Springs came over to help decorate. Fresh bread and a dessert from the bakery would round out the meal.

She almost opened a bottle of red wine to make their lunch celebratory. Why not? Because it is only lunchtime. That's why not. Who was she and what had they done with her sensible self? She would save it for tomorrow night. Lost in the chopping and adding of ingredients while she watched the movie, an hour had gone by and the aroma of the delicious soup was filling the room. Not to mention the most amazing smell of all, the bread reheating in the oven.

She hadn't paid attention and just realized that Dan wasn't inside yet. What could have kept him outside this whole time? She went out and found him high on a ladder adding lights to the eaves. She couldn't believe what he had been up to. More lights adorned her home than ever before. He'd also cut more greenery off the bottom of the tree and wound it around the stairway and porch railings.

"Wow, thanks, I can't wait to see this once it's dark out. What a wonderful surprise. My house hasn't been this decked out in years. As in ever."

He saw her appreciation and knew deep down what everyone knows. Giving really is better than receiving. Making someone else happy. That truly is what it's all about.

"Come down off that ladder," she called. "Lunch is ready."

Taking off his coat and hanging it on the hallway hook, he stomped the snow off his boots and onto the hallway rug. As he smelled the soup and bread, he remarked, "Lunch smells really good! Soup? Have you been holding out on me?"

"Maybe a little. Minestrone. It's one of three things I actually cook."

Taking his first spoonful, he looked at her with a serious expression. Her face fell. She knew she wasn't the chef that he was, but she always thought this soup was tasty. And that it would warm him up from the inside out after he had spent all that time outside. He had been feeding her delicious meals for a month and she couldn't even pull together a good pot of soup.

"You don't like it."

"Just the opposite. Is there any way I can have this recipe for the café? It's the best minestrone I've ever had."

"I would be honored. Sure!" Now, that was more like it.

"What other talents are you hiding from me?"

The rest of the day was quiet, but in a nice way. She wrapped presents while he relaxed on her couch to watch the football game on tv. She could get used to this new life.

Her mom was enjoying an easy Sunday afternoon as well, curled up on the couch alongside Jack, listening to Christmas music softly playing while they warmed up by the fire. They had taken a long walk in the snow that morning. Such a rare opportunity for North Carolinians.

Jack had moved there without giving a thought to leaving snow behind, but it was a delightful surprise to Maggie. They had walked by so many little ones out trying to gather enough snow for snowmen or snowball fights. Some of those kids had never even experienced snow before.

Now that they were back inside, she started wondering about what he would do for the holiday.

"How do you and your girls celebrate on Christmas?" she asked him.

"They get together with their in laws on Christmas Eve and I get the pleasure of watching J.J. open his gifts on Christmas day. I spend the day at

Jen's and Susan and her husband join us as well. Hey, how would you like to spend Christmas with us this year?"

"Only if you agree to join me on Christmas Eve as my guest for the village party."

"I can't think of anything I would rather do," he squeezed her hand.

He decided now would be a good time to tell her that he wanted to move out of the apartment. This was going to be a permanent move and he needed a place where he could relax, enjoy the outdoors, maybe throw a fishing line in a watering hole.

"Maggie, I'm looking at a house on a pond about three miles out of town on Beacon Highway. I was hoping you might come take a look at it with me. I would really like your opinion," he suggested.

"I love looking at houses. Just let me know when," she replied.

RECIPE

Minestrone

- 2 T olive oil

- 1 large chopped Vidalia onion

- 1 large chopped red pepper

- 1/3 c chopped celery

- 4 finely diced garlic cloves

- Sea salt to taste

- T chopped fresh rosemary

- Black pepper and red pepper flakes to taste

- 4 c organic vegetarian broth

- 1 15.5 oz can cannellini beans

- 2 c diced tomatoes, fresh or canned

- 1 ½ c chopped zucchini or yellow squash

- Package of fresh spinach

- Smallest box of orzo, cooked

- Plenty of shredded fresh parmesan

Directions: I often double this because I agree with Kate that it's even better the next day.

- If you double it, use the biggest pot you have.

- Heat the oil in a big pot over medium heat. Add the onion, red pepper, celery, garlic, sea salt, rosemary, and pepper. Stir once in a while for about 10 minutes.

- Add the broth and a cup of water, beans, tomatoes and zucchini or summer squash and simmer on low about 10 minutes. Stir in the spinach (Keep pushing it down, it'll shrink) and simmer until they wilt.

- Add as much orzo as you like, and as much parmesan.

- Top your bowl with parmesan and enjoy!

Chapter 23

Monday morning came and with it, finally, the day before Christmas Eve. The day flew by with Kate teaching her line up of three yoga classes. So many students brought in thoughtful gifts. She received candles, essential oils, bath bombs, bath salts, books. They all knew her well. She appreciated the presents, but honestly just having them choose Beacon Yoga as their community and add so much with their presence, they more than adequately filled her life with so much grace. As she and her mom closed for the night, they were happy to anticipate the rare day with no classes to be held tomorrow. The studio was going to be readied for the village party.

Maggie and Jack scored an open appointment to look at the house in the country. It was either now or after the new year, and he was eager to go look at it with her now. He wanted her with him to sense her reaction when he first went inside. The property was fenced, with a non-presumptuous gate opening onto a gravel lane that snaked up the hill, the driveway at least a quarter mile long, away from the highway. As they reached about half way to the house, they were excited to see the pond with deciduous and evergreen trees reflecting in the still water. A well-worn short dock jutted out at one point, with an old blue fishing boat tied up, bobbing in the water at its side.

The home itself was stone, covered with a red tin roof slanting down over a porch that encompassed the entire front of the house. The oak front door was massive, opening out onto the porch, and to the left and right were French doors that also could be opened to the porch.

"Nothing like a porch swing out on a porch like this, is there?" Maggie asked Jack. "I can just imagine the breeze that blows through here in the summer."

"I can too, and did you see that pond?"

The realtor was just pulling up the drive himself.

"Welcome, you two. Great location, huh?"

"Can't wait," Jack answered, "to see if the inside is as good as it is out here."

The realtor opened the lock box and Jack and Maggie were not disappointed. Boasting an open floor plan, the interior was at once welcoming and rustic. As they continued the tour, Jack found himself feeling at home there. He liked what he saw in the comfortable, light filled home. Maggie could see him in a place like this. The realtor told him not to worry if he wanted to take a few days to decide. Nothing was going to happen on Christmas anyway. Jack decided to give himself a few days to mull it over.

Around then, Jenny and Chris arrived at Kate's house at the same time as she did. Once inside she reheated the soup and set out the warmed bread and the chilled block of butter. The bottle of red wine she had wisely and patiently decided to save for tonight was open on the counter to breathe, however wine breathed. What a silly thing. Dan started playing Christmas music on her old stereo and they all relaxed for the first time that day as they listened to Bing Crosby and Andy Williams, blasts from the past, old vinyls that had once been her grandparents'.

"I'm so glad that Chris's parents could sit for the boys while we decorate tonight," Jenny mused. "Adam and Tyler are wound so tightly for Santa's arrival tomorrow night. It's a madhouse at our place."

"Well, it's quiet here. So, come have a seat, put your feet up on the coffee table, and enjoy a glass of red wine and some minestrone." Nothing was so precious in her house that they needed to be careful about spilling or making a mess and she always wanted her place to feel like a second home to her friends. I made it yesterday so now that the flavors have blended, it should be pretty tasty. Dig in."

"This is delicious," Chris declared as they sat in the living room and kept it casual. Dan agreed and said it would definitely be on the winter menu at Ivy Café. They teased Kate for holding out on the matter of her own cooking skills.

After dinner they began decorating, the guys untangling the lights and placing them around the fir as Kate and Jenny unwrapped the ornaments and hung them carefully. Kate often laughed or shared a sentimental story about an ornament she'd had since childhood. Her mom scoured the craft shows and gave her a meaningful decoration to commemorate something special each year. Before they knew it, they were throwing tinsel on the tree, and even more on each other. They could not be having more fun as the four of them were more covered in the silver strands than the tree itself.

Just then the doorbell rang. She and Dan shared a glance of 'whoever could be there?' The two of them reached the door, and as Dan opened it, Kate stood just behind him.

"Belinda," Dan said to the woman at the door, "what ---?"

The beautiful woman smiled at the two of them as Dan and Kate stood on her front porch with their mouths agape. Kate knew she was considered cute, had fresh faced girl next door looks, but Belinda looked NYC model beautiful. Dressed from head to toe in winter white, her long dark hair cascaded in soft waves out of her cashmere headband. Her makeup looked professionally applied. And her bearing was as graceful and poised as could be.

"Hello," the beautiful stranger said, "I'm Belinda, I'm sure you must be –"

Kate interrupted, "Belinda, come inside out of the cold," as she backed out of the entry and stumbled over to her best friend.

"Jenny," Kate grabbed her hand and stammered, yanking on her arm, "Come into the kitchen with me?"

"Of course." Jenny got right up and allowed Kate to pull her along, wondering who could have been at the door to alter Kate's mood so drastically.

Jenny pleaded with her once the two were alone in the kitchen.

Kate filled her in and the pieces fell together in Jenny's mind.

"It's...I can't believe I'm saying this but it is Belinda, someone Dan was with in New York. I don't know anything about her except that she is stunningly beautiful and she is on my front porch. I can't begin to compete with her for his affection. She's classy, sophisticated, gorgeous, oh my gosh. I was such a fool thinking he would fall back in love with me. After all these years."

This wasn't good. Not at all. Jenny wrapped her arms around her sweet friend. "I'm sure there is some explanation, but I can't think of why she would show up on your porch tonight either. What I do know is he has been falling in love with you all over again, that is if he ever stopped loving you. I know it, Kate, and you must too. You have to believe that. And you may not be New York City sophisticated, but who says you aren't exactly right for Dan? I know you are."

Meanwhile Dan had practically pushed Belinda back out onto the porch. He didn't really want to bring her inside. Why did his dad have to stir things up like this? Why couldn't he have left well enough alone? He'd hoped since they'd made it through the weekend without her showing up, that she had decided to leave him alone after all. But no such luck. He could only imagine what Kate must be thinking and feeling.

"Belinda, you've got it all wrong coming here," he stammered. "We've been over for a long time. I have strong feelings for Kate. I don't think I ever got over her." In the glow of the porch light Belinda grabbed his arm and he reached for hers in an attempt to pull her away from him.

"I still love her," he said.

Belinda responded by drawing him towards her in an embrace. He didn't exactly shove her but he definitely drew back. Looking her directly in her eyes, Dan firmly told her, "You have to go, Belinda."

And what Kate heard and saw as she approached them from inside was the two of them reaching for each other as Dan was saying 'I still love'... I never got over'... She flew away back to the kitchen.

"He still loves... I-- I-- I've got to go." Her friend tried to stop her but Kate was already summoning Freddie and running out the door, leaving her best friends alone at her house.

Outside on the porch, as Dan was trying to get her to leave, Belinda made her way inside and announced herself to their best friends. He stood behind her, realizing as he scanned the room that Kate wasn't there. He felt helpless and embarrassed, mostly for Belinda. She was making a fool out of herself and him. The evening was turning into a nightmare.

Gathering his wits, Dan ushered Belinda back onto the porch.

"Please leave, you have the wrong idea altogether. I wish only the best for you. I truly do, but you never should have shown up here, and..." He managed to say, "We. Are. Over."

Guiding her to her rental car, "I really am sorry," he gently offered.

She glared at him, disgust on her face, "You sure are, you're a sorry man in a sorry little house in a sorry little town. You always were."

And with that, she slid into the car, slammed the door, started the engine and roared out of the driveway, out of his life. He could only hope, for good.

Returning to the house, he ran into Jenny alone in the doorway.

She answered the unasked question she saw in his eyes.

"She left, Dan. Let her be for tonight. It'll be okay."

Kate had run home to her mom; Maggie wrapped her arms around Kate as she cried and explained what had transpired between tears.

"Oh, Katie girl, I think you misunderstood. I know love when I see it. And he loves you. I'm sure of it. As sure as I am about anything. You two are meant for each other."

"Sit down with me for a moment. Here in the kitchen. Put your feet up," she handed her a box of tissues and started boiling a kettle full of water for some chamomile tea. Her mom got out the mugs, put tea bags in them, and sat down while they waited for the water to boil. She drew a blanket around her daughter's shoulders.

"I have put this off for twelve years, but you are ready to hear it now. Honey, there are two types of men as far as I can tell. Men like your father, and men like Dan." She got up and poured the water over the tea bags and set a mug down in front of each of them.

"I think it's time you knew the full story. Your dad and I were a high school romance. I know you know that much already. You remember I was privy to yours and Dan's relationship. I had a bird's eye view. So, I know how sweet and real your friendship was. Your dad and I were a different story. If Dan had been a young man like your father, I would have kicked him to the curb. By then I could sniff those guys out. I couldn't when I was a teenager. Before I tell you more," she took a long sip of her tea and sighed, "I want you to know your dad loves you, and I'm grateful we were married. As I have told you a zillion times, I wouldn't have you otherwise."

"Mom, you're scaring me."

"No, honey, it's nothing that scary. He just wasn't faithful. The first time was in high school. I had the flu, and there was a school dance. I didn't really mind that he went, I sure didn't expect him to come over to my house while I was contagious. But I also didn't expect him to make out with

Joanie French at the party afterwards. And no one told me. I didn't find out until the next summer and by then he apologized like a crazy person until I believed he hadn't meant anything by it. Like a crazy person, I forgave him. Worse yet, I believed him."

"Oh, Mom, you must have felt awful."

"I did, but not as bad as I felt when there was a similar incident with one of my bridesmaids two weeks before our wedding. That time I didn't believe him or her. And she was no longer a bridesmaid, needless to say. But I still married him. I was so young, only twenty-two, and the idea of cancelling the wedding just didn't seem like a feasible option. Your grandparents had spent so much money. I was going to be ashamed, reasons that sound silly now, but then -- I remember the pit in my stomach as I walked down the aisle toward him, on your sweet grandfather's arm. I just felt like it was too late. The next time I knew about his cheating was the time he left for good." Kate and Maggie were both crying now. The tea had grown cold. "Katie girl, Dan is the other kind of man. The faithful kind. Let's run you a bath and you can soak some of this worry away."

Kate soaked in the bath prepared for her by her strong, amazing mom, and she appreciated that her mom had finally confided in her. But she was feeling like she'd never want to leave the bath, let alone see anyone, especially Dan. She just knew what she heard. And she was as sorry for her mom as she could be. But her mom, so sadly, was wrong about Dan. She didn't think he would cheat on her. But what was he doing, pretending to love her, stringing her along? She wished he'd never come home, that he had just stayed with Belinda in the first place. That he hadn't made her fall in love with him again. Again! He had been a kind young man.

Now she thought he was again. Wrong.

He was in love with her ten years ago. Now he still loved Belinda. His feelings for her were not at all what she had thought they were. She was right to feel that the first day that she saw him back. He was a great pretender. She had no idea why he had been toying with her. He never should have left New York or that woman he loved. Belinda the beautiful.

How could she have let herself fall so deeply for him again?

Chapter 24

Finally, she managed to climb out of the tub, towel off and put on her pajamas before crawling into her childhood bed, pulling the comforter up to her chin, and eventually falling into a light sleep that left her tossing and turning fitfully most of the night. She awoke, reached over out of habit and checked her cell for any messages that may have come in during the night. Wow, why would Dan call her, what eight times, when it was over. Seeing and hearing what she'd seen and heard was enough. She deleted the messages without bothering to read them. Christmas Eve. The party was tonight. Thank God everything she had to do was already done. No way was she going to the party tonight. She was not leaving this bed. Maybe all day. Maybe all week. Not for the foreseeable future. She snuggled closer to Freddie.

"Hey," Jenny was cautiously peeking in and opening the bedroom door. "I took the liberty of getting you this dress for the party tonight."

Kate looked up at the stunning red dress. "Oh my gosh, Jenny. You went to Greenland's and bought the dress we saw in the window. So beautiful and so thoughtful. The dress was off the shoulder, fitted with a princess neckline and tea length with a matching wrap. But I'm not going. I can't. How could I have ever believed in him, in us, again?"

"Ok. Kate. Now listen to me. I talked with Dan. He said he left you several messages. We have been friends for too long for you not to hear me out. And I can't remember ever asking you to trust me like I am now. First you are going to go try on this dress and then you have to listen to the truth."

Christmas Eve was beautiful, cold but not so cold that the event would be hampered in any way. The forecast even called for a chance of snow, but no one got too excited about that. Most people assumed the weather forecasters were just trying to give them hope. They seemed to predict it every year and it never snowed on Christmas Eve.

Maggie stood back with Jack and enjoyed the sight of lifelong friends mingling in the festive party atmosphere. Across the street, Santa's station was set up picture perfect with children in line to climb up on his lap for their wishes to be whispered in his ear. The kids felt special because they knew they were the last ones in the world to make their requests before he got on his sleigh, which was parked just a few feet away, waiting patiently to fly around the world.

A heated tent was set up for the kids to play during the rest of the party as they enjoyed games and hot chocolate or juice, mini pizzas and just a few cookies. High school kids who had enjoyed the party when they were little volunteered to oversee the younger ones.

As soon as Santa was off on his sleigh, the kids would retreat to the tent as the adults sat down to their first course of dinner. Between the serving of appetizers and the first course this year they were all excited to give Mike and Julie Riggio the proceeds from the gift-wrapping fundraiser along with the shared profits from village businesses. They had raised a little over ten thousand dollars, exceeding their wildest dreams. It seemed that everyone in town brought their gifts to the village to be wrapped this year whether they bought them there or elsewhere so they could help out the Riggio's.

Since Kate was designated to hand them the check and she hadn't shown up, Maggie had no choice but to do the honors instead. She had gathered everyone out in front of the two businesses and invited the Riggio's to join her under the awning. And as she announced the total and handed them the town's donation, Mike and Julie were not the only ones with tears in their eyes. Applause erupted and it was announced that the first course of dinner would be ready soon; guests could either eat in the cafe or the yoga studio. Jack joined Maggie for dinner, but not before guiding her under the mistletoe for a lingering kiss. They both found it incredulous to be given this second chance at happiness.

The caterers had outdone themselves and even though it felt a little weird this year to not be at Riggio's, the set up between the two businesses did work, and it was a wonderful party.

Everyone but Dan seemed to be having a great time. He was trying to put on a happy face but his smile definitely was not reaching his eyes. Why hadn't Kate at least responded to his texts and phone messages? And even if she didn't, why would she miss this party? He could not make sense of her behavior toward him. He hadn't wanted Belinda there either and he made it clear to her that it was over. Why wasn't Kate giving him a chance?

As he stood looking out at the community that he had become a part of again, he wished Kate were there. His mind drifted back to all the fun they'd had since he came home just a little over a month ago, from seeing her again out in front of the café the day he bought it, to spending Thanksgiving together, sharing meals, working on the café, and the B&B, hosting the dinner and the after caroling party, to choosing and decorating their Christmas trees. Then the disaster last night that he did not want to remember. Tomorrow was Christmas and he felt miserable.

And suddenly he looked up and there she was, a vision in red, slowly walking toward him. Their eyes locked and he walked toward her without tearing his gaze away. He took her hands in his, declaring, "I'm so sorry

I ever left, I--I don't know what you thought you heard, but I was telling Belinda to leave. That I still love you. Oh, Kate, I love you so much. I don't think I ever stopped loving you. I have this puzzle theory. Have I ever told you?"

She just shook her head no.

"I really find puzzles in so many ways reflect our lives. There's the big mess of random pieces jumbled up in the box. And the first thing we do is put the border together. We set boundaries in life just like we establish the border on the puzzle. I didn't always establish the right boundaries. And then once we put the pieces in, there always seem to be pieces that just don't fit. Sometimes, like we do with people in our lives, we try to cram them into place. And that doesn't work. We need to realize that the right pieces fit easily into place. And those are the people we want in our lives. The person I want in my life is you."

"I like that puzzle theory, Dan, and I love you too. I always have."

And finally, they kissed, the kind of kiss that is worth the wait.

As the snow started falling, the last piece of their puzzle was fixed in place.

"Kate, I want this night to be perfect in every way. I remembered what you told me on the carriage ride about the church service. Let's go over to the Methodist Church for the eleven o'clock service. I never had that experience and I want to make that memory with you tonight."

"Dan, I would love that so much!" Dan reached over and took her hand in his and as they walked over, the snow started to fall softly.

Everything was the same. And nothing was the same.

Three months later

Christmas day had been lovely and quiet, just Dan and Kate relaxing together at his place. Jack and Maggie had encouraged them to join the festivities with Jack's family, but they declined. Finally, they were together for good and they just wanted to relish the holiday. December had been hectic, often in a nice way, but they wanted to spend the holiday alone, finally together again after too many years apart.

Dan proposed on the twenty-ninth of January, the anniversary of their first date so many years ago when they were mere freshmen in high school. He invited her for dinner and made the same thing he had the first time he had cooked for her in November upon returning to Beacon.

Before she could dig in to the shepherd's pie, he presented her with a glass of bubbly and found his way to one knee.

"Will you be my forever and ever?" He gazed at her with longing and love reflected in his eyes.

"There is nowhere I would rather be and no one I would rather spend my life with," she managed as tears trailed down her cheeks. "Yes!" and she fell to her knees to embrace him. "Your mom's ring. This is incredibly special. Just perfect. I love it and I love you. I always have."

Now they were planning their summer wedding, hoping to be married in the yard at the B&B this summer. Kate and her mom were set to meet later that afternoon to start planning the big things, like choosing Kate's wedding gown. It was exciting to start planning, but Kate felt that she had everything she wanted already. She was going to just enjoy the process now.

His dad had moved to London and although things were still strained between them, Dan clung as always to a sliver of hope for future reconciliation. They would just have to see what happened in that department. One thing that gave Dan a little hope was his dad had started dating a woman he met over there and she seemed to be good for him. His edges seemed a little softer now.

Life was also going well for Maggie and Jack. They were enjoying each other's company, and taking things slowly, much of their time at Jack's home in the country. Yes, he bought it. And with Jack's financial backing, it was looking like the B&B might open by summer.

Blessings abounded in Beacon.